Forever Beth
Lost and Found

By:

Elizabeth Cook-Howard

Book One
of the
Forever Beth Series

Elizabeth Cook-Howard at:

ech@Elizabethcookhoward.com

ISBN-10:0615824838

ISBN-13:9780615824833

DEDICATION

To my sister, mother and role model -Cynthia Shirley Cook. You not only taught me how to tie my shoes but how to walk with grace.

To my nephews / brothers Jamal and Ty, No words could ever express my gratitude for sharing your mom's love.

To my children Quentin, Angelica, Joshua and Ashley my pride and joys who make me proud to be your mom every single day. Thank you for enduring the loud music, awful singing and most importantly, my playing and singing the same song over and over and over again when I write.

And last but certainly not least my husband for how many years now? Thank you for the encouragement and push.

Table of Contents

Chapter 1 – Thankful?
November 24, 1988 – Thanksgiving
Greensboro, North Carolina

Pecans from his grandparent's backyard and water, nothing more. I have about two hours of kerosene left. I better turn the heater off. My candle's brightness is coming to its end. What will I do tomorrow? No worries I tell myself for the darkness I once was afraid of as a child is being welcomed with open arms. Prepared and grateful for this allotted opportunity, I pray that the day as it is now will be the same when the darkness falls.

Bang-Bang-Bang

Bang-Bang-Bang

Awaken by the loud bangs I look at my watch, 9:52 pm. I stumble off the couch where I had been laying and inquire who is at the door.

Who is it?

Me baby, open the door.

Why did he come back? Maybe to apologize? Maybe to set right the wrong he did just yesterday? I doubt it but if I don't answer this, whatever this is will just get worse.

Michael what do you want?

I want you baby, please open the door.

Opening the door, I stand to the side. What is it Michael?

I came home to be with you. Is that okay?

Michael, how do you want me to answer that? You made it clear, I'm on my own and I prefer it that way.

On your own, hmmm *Michael burst out in a boisterous roar* Ha you on your own! Wake the fuck up and smell the coffee. You can't make it on your own. I'm all you got. Your own mama doesn't want you. Your mother and father were too eager for me to have you. And you know what… I see why.

Michael just leave, go please!

Pacing back and forth, anger emerging upon his face. No baby, you then started something and now once again I have to finish it.

God I know where this is leading. Please not tonight. Let me be spared this one time. Michael I'm sorry, apologize if you feel I'm starting anything, that isn't my intent. Can you just go please!

I'm not going anywhere. This is my mother fucking house. If you don't like that then you get the fuck out.

…………….

Go ahead

Michael opens the door and without any hesitance I get up and exit as quickly as I can. I know what is about to happen. If I can leave without anything on my feet and barely anything on my body I opt for leaving. I step out onto the porch and I'm grabbed instantly by the hair. Let the beatings begin.

You're leaving bitch? Where are you going to go? Huh? No one wants your ass.

Struggling to untangle myself from Michael's hold I begin to weep. Please let me go.

Do you understand this is my house? My castle!

Knowing my punishment was going to happen regardless, a rage begins to surface and without any control I find myself expressing how I feel about the King's castle.

Your castle? *I repeat as if his castle was a use to be and not any longer.* A castle that is in the dark? A castle without food or heat? Love that you profess with a heavy hand, a love shared with more than just me? Yes I love your castle. You're fucking castle.

Your mouth Beth… I'm warning you.

Warning me? Warning me of what? What more can you do to me?

With a smile surfacing, Smack... I warned you of that!

Hold back the tears. This will be over soon enough. But this time he will have to exhaust himself for this battle for once is going to be one to one and not the usual one vs. weak me. No this time is different. I can't control my need to fight this fight with everything I have.

What now? Something more you want to say?

I walk toward Michael with tears streaming. I pick up a candle that recently went out, hot wax swishing around due to my shaking hands. With one toss I splatter hot wax onto Michael, reaching the lower portion of his face. I then take the empty jar with all my might and throw it directly at Michael, hitting him below his nose where his mouth begins. Blood trickling down his face I'm aware of what is next. I stand in front of Michael, not moving and surprisingly no longer scared.

Bitch you just lost your mind didn't you? *Smack* Didn't you?

……………

Oh you're big and bad now huh? *Smack*

Beth for once we are not going to let this man break us, no not this time. I turn on my heel and begin to walk away but I'm pulled back into place by my ponytail.

Get the fuck over here. *Holding me now tightly with one hand around my neck.* Why do you get me like this? I tell you over and over again not to question me – not to defy me. But you continue to do so.

Do not cry, not a tear. Michael please release me now!

((What)) I don't think I heard you right *a look of amusement on his face.*

Please take your hands off me and just go. *Stay strong. We are not giving him the satisfaction of tears… No way.*

I'm here to be with my ungrateful wife and as my wife you're fucking going to listen to what I have to say. Do you understand me?

Still holding me in place by my throat Michael stop… Get off of me.

What?

((GET OFF OF ME NOW))!

Smack....... Don't ever tell me to get off what is mine.

Why did I open the door? Do not open your mouth... The hold on my neck is finally released. Michael walks toward the middle of the room.

GET YOUR ASS OVER HERE NOW!

Michael just get out and leave me the hell alone… Please!

I'm going to leave you alone alright. I'm going to make love to my wife and you're going to enjoy every second. Do you understand me?

No longer able to maintain my defiance, I begin to beg and plead. I cannot stomach the idea of this man inside me. Michael please do not… don't do this, please. *As I'm being dragged onto the couch, I begin internally to question why my life is the way it is. What had I done to warrant this? Heavenly father if you allow me to breathe another breath after this how can I continue to honor you? Please let me come home now... I beg you.*

My desperate plea to my heavenly father goes ignored. With every rapid thrust my soul is leaving me, my free will is gone. Officially as of this moment I no longer have control of self. My last nil of dignity is gone. I don't bother to question anymore how I've gotten to this place. I just be. I try to drown out his vocal expressions of enjoyment.

With tears streaming down my face I begin to hum in my head, humming over and over again no particular tune, just noise in my head to drown out this endless moment. With one last sigh and deep thrust, it is finally over. He falls from behind me and I begin to pick myself up.

Where do you think you're going?

…………

You better answer me

To the bathroom *I say in a low whisper.*

I advise you to hurry up, I'm not done.

I get up as quickly as I can and make my way to the bathroom. I sit on the toilet and begin crying uncontrollably. I hate this man so much. His touch turns my stomach. Feeling the nausea build I stand quickly and attempt to vomit but due to the lack of food, my hunger foam is all I can manage.

My face stings and my neck throbs. I can't see what damage he has done this time but I'm sure it will blend with my previous battle scars. I open the medicine cabinet to see if I have any aspirin. Feeling around, I find something even better. I sit back on the toilet and examine my prize – my precious gem. This will take care of my pain. But do I use it on him or do I use it on me. Ha, foolish, foolish girl if you use it on him your pain will still exist. Use it on yourself and darkness will proudly march in.

Finding this treasure is the sign I was looking for from God. Yes it has to be. I have no other choice I choose… me. But wait… What about daddy? Will he get through this? What are you saying of course he will! Finally he will no longer have to take sides, and the monster of a mother will no longer feel intimidated - threatened. She will finally be relinquished from her admitted mistake of carrying me to term vs a hanger. Oh yes peace shall come to him, peace will come to all.

I open the razor and pull out the blade. Using my fingers I rub the tip of the blade to insure its sharpness. Perfect! Heavenly father I ask for forgiveness not for what I am about to do to myself but for what I am doing to this innocent…… Forgive me… I ask for forgiveness for all the sins I have brought upon myself. I ask for forgiveness for the act I'm about to endure. Please allow me into your kingdom, I beg.

With tears streaming down my face I begin to wonder, if I cut my inner thigh will the darkness come sooner? Let's try… slice… ha ha…. blood begins to ooze. Slice… my left wrist done… I begin to feel sleepy… slice…I cut my right wrist….I feel so tired…. As I begin my departure I close my eyes and think of a happier place, happier time. I begin to fantasize of a different life with a mother who loved me and a father not torn between two. I envision myself with a husband who adores me as I him. I see myself holding my little girl, but all is now cloudy and disappearing… I close my eyes and begin reciting the words to an old gospel song:

Precious Lord, take my hand
Lead me on, let me stand
I'm tired, I'm weak, I'm lone
Through the storm, through the night
Lead me on to the light
Take my hand precious Lord, lead me home

When my way grows drear precious Lord linger near
When my light is almost gone
Hear my cry, hear my call
Hold my hand lest I fall
Take my hand precious Lord, lead me home
When the darkness appears and the night draws near
And the day is past and gone
At the river I stand
Guide my feet, hold my hand
Take my hand precious Lord, lead me home

Heavenly father I now close my eyes and wait for complete darkness. I wish for peace, peace finally to everyone burden by me.

Chapter 2
My Happy - June 26, 1999

Knock …… Knock

Who is it?

Rosa it's Beth Morris

Opening the door Hi Beth, I was expecting to see you tomorrow.

I know… sorry, but I have something small for Rosie. I was hoping she could wear it tomorrow, her big day and all.

Beth please come in *I step into the apartment.* Rosie is still at school but you can wait if you want?

No… I have other visits today. I just wanted to drop this off. *In my hand I open a small box containing a sterling silver charm bracelet. I pull the bracelet out of the box.* Okay, five charms representing her most favorite people and things. A kitten for pickles, a hamster for McDonald, ballerina shoes for the obvious, Hello Kitty just because and last but certainly not least, most favorite "mom".

Rosa's eyes fill with tears… Thank you she will love it but you shouldn't have.

Of course I did… *because that little girl means more to me than anyone will ever know.*

She will wear this proudly *Rosa says as she wipes away the tears.*

Fighting back my own tears... Six years...... six years......

Yes and we both are alive and healthy. *Rosa trying to hold back her emotions.*

Stop it I tell myself, no tears. You should be proud of yourself. You're a fantastic mom.

Look at us, we're weeping over a six year old Kindergarten graduation.

Ha ha ...I know, but this one is ever so special. So I will see you both at the school tomorrow at 10?

Yes and Beth Thank...

Do not complete that sentence *I should be thanking you...* I'll see you both in the morning. And oh, I ordered a cake hope that's ok.

Mrs. Morris, I knew you would. For six years for every occasion Rosie... *Rosa fighting back tears* I knew you would. Thank you.

See you tomorrow. *Walking back to my car I notice the time. Oh crap... I have to get to Queens in 20 minutes. Baisley... I'll take Linden Blvd. Once in the car I begin strolling through the channels on the radio. Ah, Mary J. Do she ever sing about un-*

painful love? Ha ... Yup she's singing about me once again. Your sick humor Mrs. Morris I tell myself!

Finally arriving to my next appointment, I'm at least 20 minutes late due to traffic. Okay Beth you know the routine, poker face. No other emotions. You would think after seven years I would feel more comfortable but so far no such luck.

Good Afternoon… I'm here to see Angela Black……

Can I see some ID?

Oh crap why do I always come unprepared Yes I have. Sorry please give me a second *I begin looking through my purse.*

Sure I have all day.

What the fuck, attitude... Find you're damn identification so you can go on about your business. Here it is… *presenting to the eye rolling bitch behind the desk.*

Room 414, and tell her to come downstairs to get her mail. We don't deliver.

Sure? *But if you got your ass off that stool maybe, just maybe your ass wouldn't be the size of Cuba!*

Making my way to the elevator I take in the lack of motivation circling the air. I hate coming to this place. I step into the elevator and the stench of urine hits my nose, trash on the floor. This is what the City of New York confirms as a family shelter. This place is no better than EAU! I make my way to room 414.

Knock… Knock

Who is it?

Hi, Ms. Black My name is Beth Morris… I'm with Care House.

What?

I'm with Care House. Could you please open the door?

Now isn't a good time.

Ms. Black I came all this way. Please can I speak with you briefly regarding services?

Click... Door opens

Hi Ms. Black *Beth take your mind off it. Look the woman in her face but stay stoned face, stay focus* I'm with Care House. I came to review services and to see how we could assist you and your children.

I don't need any help.

Well before you say that, can I review what we could offer and how I possibly could assist?

Do what you want……

Stepping into the unit, the stench of dirty diapers hits my nose immediately. I begin to scan the one room unit. Four children all under the age of five and an adult sharing this four by four size room. Food crumbs everywhere. Ugh… The couch / bed stained with I don't want to know.

You can sit if you want.

No, no thank you Ms. Black. I had a long drive over and was stuck in traffic so sitting right now…

Whatever

So, how old are the kids?

I don't know… I'm sure you can find out. Why are you here again?

I'm here to see how things are going with you and how Care House could be of assistance.

I don't need help *and as Ms. Black continues her attempts to shorten this visit, two little boys run over to where she is sitting.*

Mommy, mommy I hungry……

Take your ass back to the couch. I don't want to hear another word. Do you hear me?

Smiling I look at the two boys then the twin girls sleeping in a pack and play. Ms. Black, you have beautiful children and your twin girls, how old are they?

The girls are six months.

They are beautiful! You're very blessed.

What? *Cocking her head to the side*

You are blessed, blessed with four beautiful children.

Yeah well blessed isn't what I would call it.

Hey little man what's your name? *Such sadness in his eyes.*

………….

He doesn't talk much. He receives services.

Oh, you look about four *I hold up four fingers.*

With a smile he shakes his head yes.

And would you be Tyrone? *Yes I think the report stated Tyrone oldest son four – just turned four.*

He shakes his head again, this time with a bigger smile.

You know Tyrone I may have a coloring book in my bag with hmmm a few crayons. Would you like to color?

Tyrone's eyes widen even more and without hesitance, put his hands out.

Here you go little man. Now I'll make a deal with you. If you sit and color me a picture while I talk to your mom, I may have a small surprise.

With anticipation, Tyrone goes back to the couch with his brother. I turn my attention back to Ms. Black.

Look Mrs. Morris, I don't know what you want or what you want me to say.

Ms. Black I'm just here to make sure you're okay. I already have a report regarding what happened, nothing more needs to be said. If and when you want to talk about it we will. Until then how can I assist you?

Surprised, Ms. Black physically seems a bit relieved. Her body language instantly becomes more relaxed.

How many sessions has Tyrone missed?

With a confused look, Ms. Black looks at me.

Excuse me?

How many speech sessions did he miss? *Asking again but rephrasing.*

Two or three. Brenda his teacher was coming twice a week.

So he is under the Committee for Pre-School Special Education?

Yes, he recently aged out of Early Intervention.

Ok. Do you have Brenda's number? I will call and schedule her to come here and meet with Tyrone.

Not sure if annoyed or confused, Ms. Black's response is delivered with a stare. Brenda can come here?

Yes. Just until we find you and the kids a more permanent place Brenda should come here. I will work it out with the shelter.

Thanks *more of a question then a statement.*

What's the number?

Whisking through papers in her purse, Ms. Black writes the telephone number down on a piece of paper and hands it to me.

What about clothing?

We have a few things.

Okay, make a list of the items you need and I will see what I can do. Let me have the sizes for you and the kids.

I don't need anything for myself.

Hey that's your answer today, right now. But maybe an hour from now, maybe tomorrow you might feel differently *I say with a smile. I lean towards Ms. Black and whisper* the black eye, scratches and hand print will go away. You will regain your self-respect and dignity. When this happens you will be ready to head out again.

Looking relieved that the elephant in the room has finally been noticed, Ms. Black gives a half smile Can I get you a drink Mrs. Morris?

First please call me Beth and no thank you, I need to get going. But can I come back tomorrow morning?

Ah, sure.

Great how about 9:00? I know it is early but I have a special graduation to attend later in the morning. *Turning toward Tyrone and his brother...* Hey Tyrone my picture ready?

With a nod, Tyrone comes over and hands me the picture.

Wow this is great. Can I take this with me?

Another nod

Well I can't take this picture without giving you something. So let's see what I have with me.

Searching my purse. Hmmm, do you like Sponge Bob?

Tyrone's eyes light up and he shakes his head yes.

Oh thank goodness because all I have in my bag are cookies shaped like Sponge Bob, Patrick, Squidward and you may even find Sandy.

Tyrone begins to laugh and grabs for the box of graham cookies. Before releasing I turn to Ms. Black for approval. With a nod yes I give Tyrone the box.

Alrighty then… Ms. Black I will see you tomorrow at nine.

Please call me Angela and as to sizes, 12 for me, Tyrone is a 6x, the girls12 to 14 months and Malcolm a 4.

With a smile I turn and reply great I will see you tomorrow morning.

Chapter 3
How the Day Ends

Shit, Look at the time. The only time I will ever be on time ironically will be for my own damn funeral. Okay I can drop these things off with Ms. Black and then head to the school. Why am I so nervous? Funny you would think she was my... No she's not. Don't go to that place Beth... Do not go! Happy thoughts, only happy thoughts today!

Arriving to Baisley Shelter, I grab all the bags, trying to make a single trip to save time. Oh good grief Cuba ass is still sitting in the same spot.

Good Morning, I'm here to see Ms. Black.

Who?

Oh why is this bitch playing this game? Ms. Black in room 414! I was here yesterday.

Oh yeah, didn't I tell you to tell her to get her mail?

Beth, keep it together, do not snap. Yes you did ah… your name?

Well the pile is still sitting down here.

My request for her name completely ignored. Listen Cuba A… *you just did not say that* I apologize, my error. I did not relay the message yesterday but please allow me, I will deliver the mail to her myself. *Because lord knows your big ass isn't going to get up and give it to her.*

No it's against the rules. She needs to come down here.

Well in case I neglect to inform her again I suggest that you or someone else go up and inform her. I'm pretty sure some rule regarding the mail is in place. Better yet, I will call Sister Diane myself and inquire about the mail. *Stupid bitch....*

Ah… No I will take care of it.

I thought so. Lord knows Sister Diane is the evilest Nun I ever met. Ha I guess Sister Diane scares the holy shit out of Cuba ass too.

I head to the elevator trying not to drop anything. One would assume that Cuba ass would have at least offered to help. Okay 414

Knock… Knock…

Who is it?

Hi Ms. Black - Angela it is Beth Morris.

Click... door opens Good Morning Mrs. Morris.

Is this the same woman I met with yesterday? Good Morning. You look like the sun is shining today.

With a smile Yes it certainly is a good day. *In a whispering tone,* a little makeup goes a long way.

Well you look wonderful. I'm sorry that I can't stay long but here are a few things for the kids. Hope you don't mind but I included a few toys and healthy snacks for the boys.

No… thank you very much.

Oh and this bag is for you.

Ms. Black opens the bag and begins pulling out the items. For me?

Yes for you. If the shoes don't fit let me know and I will exchange. I took a guess, seven and a half. So when you're ready you have a few outfits for running errands, doctor appointments etc.

Ms. Black continues looking through the bag. You didn't miss a beat. Deodorant, perfume… Thank you very much.

You're more than welcome. Unfortunately I have to head out but you have my card. If you need anything more please let me know. *Walking toward the door to leave I realize I didn't review my contact with Tyrone's Speech Therapist. I stop short.* Oh, I spoke with Brenda and she said she had your cell number and will call you with a schedule.

Yes she called last night and said she spoke with you.

Great and one more thing, the friendly security guard downstairs wanted me to remind you that you have mail. *Better yet, the evil bitch downstairs is too lazy to get off her ass and inform you of the mail being held at the front desk.*

With a smirk and as if she just read my mind, Ms. Black replies with a chuckle... Yes I will go down shortly.

Great, alright then, I will see you next week.

Thank you again Mrs. Morris.

No thanks needed, but you are more than welcomed.

Driving on the Interboro Parkway, an overwhelming feeling hits. Oh it's just your nerves Beth. I can't be late to this. Six years, wow where did the time go? Six years and they both are healthy. My eyes begin to swell. No I will not cry I will not cry! Convincing myself not to be so emotional lasted no more than a few minutes, until I arrive to Rosie's school. Perfect, a parking space right in front.

Entering the building I hear the class singing We've Only Just Begun. Lordy Beth, fight the tears. I make my way to the auditorium and sit toward the middle. I begin scanning for Rosa. Where is she? I then look and scan the graduates in their caps and gowns. How adorable but I don't see Rosie. She's here I just can't tell them apart. The principal stands and begins the roll call of the graduates. Let me get the camera ready. Okay they are up to the M's, here we go.

((Rosie Morales))

I begin to cheer and holler, Yea… Rosie. *But in the midst of my cheering I notice no Rosie... No Rosa cheering along. Something is wrong, very wrong... Rosa would not miss this day. She would have Rosie here on a gurney. I head down to where the class is sitting and gently tap Rosie's teacher on the shoulder.*

Ah excuse me Mrs. Greenburg, Rosie didn't come to school today?

Mrs. Greenburg turns around to face me Hi Beth, no she didn't. You haven't heard from Rosa?

Not since yesterday. I told her I would meet her here at 10:00.

When I saw Rosa yesterday she was very excited about today. I'm concerned. No way would she or Rosie would have missed this.

I agree. Okay I'm going to head over to the home.

Please call me from the home just to confirm everything is okay.

I will. *Something is wrong, very wrong. Please God let them be okay. The last report, both of their counts were fine, counts so low for Rosa, she is able to decrease a few of the antiviral medications. Please God just let everything be okay, let them both be okay.*

Driving up to Rosa's apartment building that overwhelming feeling comes over me once again. I'm going to be sick. Three police cars and two ambulances in front of the building. Think positive Beth, they both are fine... Stay calm.

I park about a half a block away. Walking toward the building I internally begin to pray, asking God to protect them and to let them both be okay. I make my way through the crowd, making my way to the area taped off by police. What in the hell could be wrong?

About to enter the area cut off by police I'm stopped by a uniformed officer.

Excuse me Miss but you cannot go in.

My name is Beth Morris and I work with one of the families in the building.

Name of the family?

Rosa, Rosa Mora… *and before I could finish my words I hear a whaling scream, a cry from a familiar voice. I know that voice. It's Jasmine, Rosa's sister. My knees buckle. The officer catches me by the waist and puts me back onto my feet.*

Miss are you alright? Miss…

I can't speak. I attempt to put myself upright. What happened? Is Rosie and Rosa okay? Can I go in?

Sorry Miss you cannot.

Please I beg you. Please! *As I'm pleading, tears begin to stream down my face. Overhearing my desperate plea, a Detective walks over.*

Excuse me ma'am, my name is Detective Walker, I'm with the 72nd precinct. Can you tell me how you know the family?

In a daze, I try to answer but I can't keep focus. What happened?

Ma'am, are you alright? Can you tell me how you know the family?

I'm a case worker with Care House.

And you worked with the deceased?

My legs completely buckle, I fall to my knees. Deceased? Who is the deceased? *I ask but already know the answer.*

Looking confused, Detective Walker extends a hand to hoist me up. Once steadied on my feet he continues Ms. Morales and her daughter were found…

And as Detective Walker continues to talk my mind goes blank, unable to comprehend what he is saying. This can't be happening. I just saw her yesterday. This is a joke, a very bad joke, bad dream.

Ma'am, are you okay?

Laughing with tears streaming down my face This is a joke isn't it? This isn't happening……

While Detective Walker continues to try to grasp my attention I feel arms hugging me ever so tight. I feel wetness on my shoulder.

Beth, they are gone… They are gone, no longer with us.

What?

Both of them are gone.

How? I was just at the school waiting for them.

They are gone *and as Jasmine says* they are gone *once more, I see the stretchers coming out of the building. One then two! My world just crumbled.*

I managed to get myself home. How, I don't know. I don't even remember driving the car. But I'm here now alone in this apartment and now alone in the world. The life I managed to live over the past six years just ended. What's left? Right now only one self-proclaimed pleaser could take this pain away, make some sense of the here and now.

I walk into the kitchen and pull a bottle of vodka from the cabinet. It's been a long time Mr. Absolute. How wonderful you look. The only man in my life that can please me like no other! *I begin to chuckle with tears falling.* Yup Mr. Absolute your one good fucking man.

I walk to the couch with Mr. Absolute in one hand and a glass in the other. I sit, pour and begin my indulgence with an old friend. Gulping shots of straight vodka, I begin to remember how I met Rosa. How I finally found unconditional love.

April 01, 1992

Tap… Tap…

Come in

Hi Beth, I'm heading to St. John's hospital. We received a call from the ER regarding a 22 year old woman who was severely injured. You should find a written report on the fax. Take five minutes to review and we will head out.

We? *Looking very puzzled*

Yes we! However, you will be the lead on this one.

What? *My stomach is in my throat.* Rochelle I'm not ready to do this on my own?

We are shorthanded and you're more than ready to open a case on your own.

Rochelle I don't think I'm rea…

Before I could complete my sentence, Rochelle interrupts You're more than ready.

I go to the fax, grab the report and head out with Rochelle.

On the way I review the report. Twenty- two year old Hispanic female with three broken ribs, head contusion and broken nose. Assaulted by live- in boyfriend after being informed of positive HIV results by way of prenatal blood screen. Patient fourteen weeks pregnant. Holy fuck!

When we arrive to St. John's Hospital, my nerves kick in. I'm not ready to do this. Rochelle, the leader that she is takes charge.

Excuse me my name is Rochelle Horowitz with Care House. I'm looking for a Rosa Morales?

The nurse behind the desk eyes the id tag hanging around Rochelle's neck. Bed three.

Can you please page Barbara White, Director of Social Work and let her know I'm here?

Sure… *Over the intercom,* Barbara White please call the ER. Barbara White please call the ER.

Rochelle thanks the nurse and turns to me. Ready?

With a blank stare I reply, I guess.

You will do just fine. She's in bed 3.

I begin asking God to help me as I walk to bed three. Hi Ms. Morales *laying on her side with her back toward me, Ms. Morales rolls over to face me. When she looks in my direction my eyes begin to swell. What the fuck!* My name is Beth Morris. I'm a case worker with Care House. *Oh God please let me get through this, please.* I've secured emergency housing for you. I was told you are being discharged?

Ms. Morales nods yes and attempts to whisper. I can leave now.

Well then let's get you ready. *Her movement very slow, I begin assisting with putting her clothing on. As she struggles to take off the hospital gown her petite frame becomes a walking exhibit, showing the proof of her abuse. Then sadly as she turns to her side her pregnancy silhouette is pronounced. How could anyone beat a woman knowing she is expecting, carrying a child? As quickly as I entertain the question is as quickly as I answer my own question.*

Do you have anyone you want to call?

She shakes her head no

Okay then, it is you and me kid... *My sick humor kicks in but in turn a small smile surfaces on Ms. Morales face.*

I pick up my glass and gulp now my fifth or sixth shot of Mr. Absolute. How can someone do this? Why? What a sick fuck. I pour another shot.

October 19, 1993

Beth you have a call on line one. It is Rosa Morales, she says it is urgent.

Okay….. Hello Beth Morris

Hi Beth it's me... Rosa

Hi Rosa is everything ok?

Ah not really, I just went into labor. I called my sister but I got her voice mail. Umm I was wondering if you…

Interrupting...Rosa my day is pretty slow here, do you mind if I come up and sit with you?

With the sound of relief, Beth I would like that very much. I'm at Mt. Sinai.

Mt. Sinai, Ok see you in a few.

Hanging up the phone Yea *I clap my hands* Paige I'm heading over to Mt. Sinai. Rosa went into labor. Can you let Rochelle know?

Sure Beth. By your excitement one would think you were the proud papa.

With a big smile I know. See you tomorrow.

When I arrive to the hospital it is a few minutes pass noon. Rosa was already taken into the OR. While in the waiting area a scrooge looking nurse walks up to me.

Are you Beth Morris?

I am

Ms. Morales ask that you come into the OR. Please follow me.

Following Nurse Ratchet I have an eagerness to run in the opposite direction, to run as far away as possible. I mean come on for peak sakes it's a c-section.

Put this on.

What the fuck!

Walking into the operating room I hear the doctor asking Rosa if she is ok. I walk to the top of the table and the doctor warns "I advise that you stay on that side of the curtain."

My nervous humor replies Doctor no worries my ass isn't moving. *Not realizing how inappropriate my response is, the room including Rosa starts to laugh*

Hey how are you feeling?

Ha ha not a damn thing.

Well I guess that's a good thing huh. *We both laugh*

Okay Rosa, you're going to feel some pressure. *Immediately after, the doctor states* she's out *and a small soft cry fills the room. In this moment my heart feels so heavy. I look over and there she is. The nurse brings her over and places her on Rosa's chest. With tears flowing, Rosa cries out* "She's so beautiful".

Trying to hold back my tears "yes she is, congratulations a little Rosie".

In a split second Rosa yells "You just named her, Rosie it is".

Now my crying is out of control. As the nurse takes Little Rosie, Rosa ask Could Beth hold her?

The nurse looking oddly at me replies, well let's get her cleaned up first.

Disappointed I turn to Rosa. I have the whole evening to hold her. Well when you don't have her *and we both laugh.*

About an hour later, Rosa is settled in her room. The nurse comes in with little Rosie. Although I immediately want to just grab and hold her, the nurse puts Rosie in Rosa's arms. The nurse then proceeds to say "Remember, no breast feeding" *then turns to me as if I understood the meaning behind her statement. As the nurse continues what sounds like a scolding I interrupt*

Rosa Could I hold her just for a second? *Rosa places Rosie in my arms. I go down to kiss Rosie's cheek and the nurse looks startled. Rosa, who looks both embarrassed and pissed responds to Nurse Ratchet's lack of decorum*

Beth what the good nurse is trying NOT to say is I'm HIV Positive and the likeness of Rosie being positive.....

In that instant, the life that was filling the room turned to a death cloud. Tears begin falling from Rosa's eyes.

"Well I have asthma so I guess we settled medical diagnosis". *I again kiss Rosie on her cheek, but this time whispering in her ear* You're going to be okay kid. *I lookup, chuckle and hand Rosie back to her mom.*

Around 6:00 p.m. Rosa's sister arrives. Introducing me to her sister Jasmine, Rosa seems nervous as to the questions her sister would have. It would've been great if she was here when Nurse Ratchet received her scolding from Rosa, that way everyone who Rosa felt should know would be informed and the matter could be put to rest.

Rosa I will be back tomorrow. *Kissing Rosa goodbye, I then head out. Walking to the elevator I check my cell phone. Six missed calls, all from Cynthia? First message - Beth it's me call me as soon as possible. Seconds message - Beth call me I really need to speak to you. Third call me ASAP.... But this message my sister's voice cracks.*

Cynthia is known as the pillar of our family, the matriarch. She does not become easily rattled. I can count the few times that she has shown any type of weakness in this area. But the protector she is, the emotions expressed immediately becomes energy / motivation to address the situation. As for the here and now only one situation could be the cause for the emotion in her voice, one factor. Imagining what that factor is I fall back against the wall and put my hands over my face with hopes of silencing the deathly cry within me. I have to face this. I can't avoid not calling her back. Quickly dialing her, Cynthia picks up after the first ring...

Beth.... Umm *her voice cracking* "Daddy passed".

From these two words my world just ended. Without saying a word I end the call. How can this be? Do not lose it here. Come on Beth, pick yourself up. You're okay. Trying to figure out my next move, what to do? Where to go? I begin walking toward the elevator. On my way I pass the nursery and there she is, little Miss Rosie. I put my head to the glass, tears flowing. Nurse Ratchet from earlier waves me in. I guess now that I know the big secret? I'm offered to sit and feed little Rosie. Any other time I would question if this was okay. Confirm with Rosa. But in this moment I don't want any confirmations or affirmations. I just needed someone to love, to hold and right now Rosie is the only person that can fulfill this need. She would have to.

Sitting in this rocker with Rosie in my arms Nurse Ratchet begins tending to another baby, timing I'm so grateful for. Tears begin to flow down my face. I can only think of my father, the man whose been by my side as much as he could allow himself to be. I know it has been hard for him. Choosing sides, trying his hardest to mend the strife between my mother and me. Trying on many occasions to correct the many wrongs set upon me. To discredit the many horrific statements made to me. I know he tried, probably trying until his last breath. My only thoughts right now are of him. I look down at Rosie and tell her how lucky she is to have the mom she has. I tell her how important unconditional love is and how lucky she is to have it. Up to a few minutes ago I did. But now I don't. My tears begin to fall faster. Looking down at Rosie I see new life, innocence. Oh how I wish I was her. How I wish I was the innocent one, brand new to the world with no pre-expectations. How I wish in this moment. As I'm rocking, Rosie opens her eyes, Hazel. She begins to suck the bottle a bit more forcefully. I pull the bottle out of her mouth to take in her complete beautiful face. She gives a small coo, her eyes close and instantly this precious little girl so new in life falls asleep. In this moment my heart seems full again, filled by a six hour old precious baby girl, Little Rosie.

Chapter 4
Welcome Old Friend

I just finished my bottle of absolute. Shit I feel soo good, too good. Time for some music! I stumble across the living room and turn on the radio.

You're listening to 98.7 Kiss FM, here's an oldie but goodie, Heat Wave and Always and Forever.

You're fucking kidding me. I hate this fucking song. I begin to sing. Each moment with you is just like a dream to me… *Shit yeah what a fucking dream, a fucking nightmare. Bastard! Every day you did love me in your own special way. Yeah you loved me alright. Baby I love you so here's a smack across your face to remember me by. Oh wait, I need you to know how much I love you so let me grab you by the throat. Perfect, a little choke mark to go with that hand print across the face. I begin to laugh. My wedding song, Always and Forever. What an appropriate song choice because I will always and forever remember it all. I will always and forever remember what your fucking low life - pathetic ass did to me. I fall onto the sofa... Oh I feel too good for a pity party. Oh yeah... Ring my bell, now that's the jam. I stagger up once again to turn the volume up louder. Trying to dance to the beat, I'm interrupted by someone banging on the door.*

"Go away"

Knock… Knock…

I said go the fuck away……

Mrs. Morris……

Knock… Knock…

Mrs. Morris it is Detective Walker … Mrs. Morris please open the door

Detective Walker who… *I stumble to the door with glass in hand. I open the door…*Can I help you? *Barely standing*

Mrs. Morris I met you earlier today……

You met me? *I say with a conniving smile. I would remember meeting such a fine piece of man. Tall, firm with oh so luscious caramel tone skin. No we haven't met.*

Yes…*As if he heard my thoughts* At the Morales's home?

My facial expression changes from oh baby I would love to have you to grief and despair. Why are you taking my buzz away? I don't want to talk about that.

Sorry Mrs. Morris but I need to ask you a few questions. I assure you, it will not take long and you can get back to *Detective Walker looks around me and set sites on the empty vodka bottle on the coffee table, my partially filled glass in hand and then directly into my eyes* get back to whatever you were doing. May I proceed? Ask a few questions?

With a chuckle I whisper, Can I ask you one? Boxers or briefs?

Both amusement and fear strikes his face. Mrs. Morris I'll come back another time.

Embarrassed and amused by his reaction I try to re-focus. No, no, no, come in, come on in. Have a seat. What would you like to know? *I stumble to the couch. Detective Walker takes a seat by the door. Ha, looks like he's afraid of little ole me.*

Mrs. Morris… Can you tell me what you know about Hector Rodriguez?

Not wanting to discuss this… How did you get my address?

Mrs. Morris? From Care House, your employer gave me your contact information.

Huh, I need to have a talk with them. I know they make jokes about me getting laid but this is going overboard, having someone come to my home? *I begin to laugh at my own words but suddenly my laugh turns into weeping... I throw my hands to my face.*

Mrs. Morris are you okay?

Back to laughing with tears falling, I shout I'm just fucking dandy, peachy.

Your husband, is he home?

In my best drunken southern accent I reply "Well I declare sir, are you asking because you have something in mind?" *I begin to laugh hysterically once again.*

Maybe I should come back *and once again Detective Walker is immediately to his feet.*

I stand to protest his leaving but suddenly the room begins to spin. Oh no, I'm about to hit the floor... Here it comes. I fall to the floor. I hear very softly

Mrs. Morris… Beth Morris are you okay?

Huh, what? *And back out I go... I drift into a drunken slumber.*

When I wake I'm in my clothes, fully dressed but in my bed? Last I remember I was on the couch. Shit what time is it? I look to my left. Oh God 7:30 in the morning. How did I get in here? When? ((Gizmo)), ((Gizmo)) *He doesn't come... This is odd, normally by 6:00 a.m. Gizmo is purring and nudging me to get up. I rise to a sit up position, ugh this feeling...... I turn to my right side table, a glass of water and a bottle of aspirin? Hmm when did I put this here? I pick up the glass of water to take a sip. What is this? A business card affixed to the side of the glass...* You will probably need this when you get up. I would like to continue my interview today. Can you please call and set up a time. Signed Detective Walker. *What the fuck?*

I stumble out of bed. My head is killing me and I feel I'm going to heave anything and everything in me. I make my way to the kitchen and find Gizmo by his bowl already eating. When did I get up to fill his bowl? Shit what did I do?

Ring… Ring…

Oh God... Shit so loud. Hello?

Hey Beth, Are you ok?

What? Who is this?

Your sister! *Stated with extreme sarcasm* are you ok?

Yes why?

A Detective Walker called last night and said I should check-in with you, that a family you were working with was murdered?

Her last statement hit me like a ton of bricks... I just remembered yesterday. I'm fine... listen I have to go.

(((BETH)))

Oh shit, her yelling What?

Beth, do not make me come over...

Oh Cynthia, I'm fine. I'll call you later.

Make sure you do... I love you

Yes I love you too.

Not even a minute later the Phone rings again....

Hello?

Hi Beth, are you okay? I called you several times last night, both on your cell and home line.

Sigh.... Hi Rochelle I'm fine. I'll see you in the office.

No, you are not working today. You're going to take a few days off. No if's and's or buts about it.

Rochelle I can't stay home *doing so will give me cause to rethink over and over again this...* I'm coming into the office. *I hang up immediately to avoid the repercussions of my blatant defiance.*

I stagger from the kitchen into the bathroom with the intent to prepare myself for work. With every movement I feel as if I'm carrying boulders on my shoulders. How am I going to make it through this day? Trying to suppress my tears from escaping, I sit on the edge of the bathtub and I begin to pray. Lord, please give me the strength to make it through this day. Give me the strength to function. Give me the strength to mask my sorrow. Give me the strength and courage to continue… Continue with life.

I arrive to the office a little after nine. Okay you can do this as long as the topic stays away from what occurred. I'll just stay to myself and get some work done. I'll focus on Ms. Black's case. Yes, maybe I can get her and the kids into a more permanent housing situation, my goal for today.

Hey Paige

What are you doing here?

Last I knew I worked here?

You know what I mean.

Look I'm fine… *Okay fine somewhat of an exaggeration but I am making it. I would continue to do okay if the questioning ceased, if everyone stopped with the questions.*

Well Rochelle requested that you go directly to her office if you came in.

Shit... I'm not up to this... Okay.

I head to Rochelle's office. Please no questions... This is all I need. I mean what is the big deal? She wasn't my child. Just another case... Do not cry, do not cry.

Tap... Tap...

Come in.

Hi, Paige said you wanted to see me?

Yes come in. You and I will have a very long discussion, but first please join us. *When I walk in, Detective Walker is standing to greet me. Shit, not now - not the questions.*

Mrs. Morris how are you?

Well, thank you. *You know damn well how I'm doing. Probably know more then you should know. Damn what did I say or do last night?*

What can you tell me about Hector Rodriguez?

He's a low life that should burn in hell?

Is that your professional or personal opinion?

Excuse me?

What Beth is trying to say *and Rochelle looks me in the eyes* he brutally attacked Rosa six years ago.

Yes I read the report on that. Has he been around lately?

Not that I know of, why? Is he the one, did he do this?

We don't know who is responsible. We are looking at all possibilities.

Well I suggest you find out what he was doing? *As the words slip through my lips Rochelle turns to me. She senses the anger building.*

Mrs. Morris can you tell me anything more? When was the last time you saw Rosa?

Oh my fucking God. Keep it together Beth, you can get through the questions I saw her the day before yesterday around 2 pm. I went to her home to bring Rosie her graduation gift. *My voice cracks.* Ahem.... *No tears, come on, you can hold it together for a few more minutes, come on* I dropped off a little charm bracelet for her to wear to graduation.

Well that was a bit generous. You do this with all the families you work with?

EXCUSE ME?

Do you?

What exactly are you asking me?

Mrs. Morris these are questions I have to ask.

Instead of wasting time with me, maybe you should get off your jelly doughnut eating ass and find out who slit a six year old throat. And while you're at it, figure out if the same fucking low life beat the shit out of her mother and stabbed her four times. Maybe that's what you need to be doing. *With tears streaming, I stand and turn to Rochelle* You know what I will take this day! *I storm out and head for my office.*

Beth I heard yelling coming from Rochelle's office. Is everything okay?

Yes just dandy Paige. Can you please make a copy of available Section Eight Housing opportunities in Queens and Brooklyn?

Sure but Beth, maybe you should separate yourself from work right now!

Thanks for the recommendation but could you please make the copy so I can take it with me!

As Paige leaves my office I sit in my chair. I begin scanning the many pieces of artwork hanging. From Easter Bunnies to Santa I must have at least forty pictures hanging all from Rosie and they all read the same "LOVE ROSIE". I take two of my favorites down and place into my briefcase.

Tap… Tap….

Come in…..

Paige enters my office with the copies I requested. Beth, do you need anything else?

No Paige but thanks *Paige continues to linger as I prepare myself to leave.* If needed you can reach me at home!

Sure Beth. I'll see you?

In a few days *I pick up my purse and briefcase and head out of the office.*

Driving home I begin to panic. Foolish - foolish woman. You're going back to an empty apartment, to sit and talk to a cat? To be held by who? Foolish girl! Yup you're going home where you will be alone. But Mr. Absolute will keep me company. To insure my company stays awhile I stop at the liquor store and purchase two more friends, Mr. Absolute one and two. My double indulgence sounding sinfully good!

Finally arriving home I grab my two new friends from the floor of my backseat. In doing so I notice a box I completely forgot about. Taking the box along with my bottles I head indoors.

Gizmo I'm home. *Gizmo runs over and rubs his head and body against my lower leg.* Yes back so soon. *I grab a glass out the cupboard and pour myself a drink. Well how about some cake, let them eat cake. I open the box. One strawberry Barbie cake... Happy K-day graduation Rosie... I take my finger and scrape Rosie's name. My eyes swell. I open and pour my first drink, taking a swig versus a sip. Oh yeah, just what I need.*

Becoming robotic, I continue to fill my glass and gulp in one sip. The more I drink the more I feel I'm in control of self and when reality begins to set in I can rely on Mr. Sandman for a few more hours of avoidance.

About an hour into my building drunken stupor I begin scanning the many photos of Rosie displayed in my apartment. Pictures from practically every outing we had, even just a walk in the park, a walk around the block. Oh how beautiful she is. My Little Rosie, from birth a smile larger than life, a smile that could melt the hearts of the sternest of stern.

With each shot I indulge in memories of my Little Rosie until I am interrupted by the phone ringing.

Hello?

…..

Hello?

Ah this is Detective Walker

You're fucking kidding me I already told you what I know.

Yes you have Mrs. Morris and even more.

The even more I guess is my doughnut statement. I can't help but to laugh... Then why are you calling me?

Mrs. Morris I'm actually outside your apartment, could I talk to you just for a minute?

You are talking to me

I know Mrs. Morris please

Without answering and without warning I hang up the phone and open the door... How can I help you?

Ah... I didn't realize you hung up *phone still to his ear.*

Well I did... How can I help you?

Can I come in?

Stepping to the side, I'm pretty sure you remember where to sit....

Ah yes I do...

Hmmm, Can I get you a drink?

No I'm on duty

Oh too bad for you. *I pour myself another shot.*

Mrs. Morris do you think having another drink is a good idea?

Who in the hell does this man think he is? My father is six feet under.... THANK YOU!

Mrs. Morris, I did not come to argue. I came to apologize for this morning. Mrs. Horowitz informed me of your involvement with the Morales family and I'm really sorry for....

I interrupt No apology needed. Just another day, another death, another....... *uncontrollably I begin to weep. I put my hands up to my face......* Just another senseless death of a precious child and a mother who would do anything.... I mean anything for her child...

Detective Walker walks over to where I'm sitting and hands me a tissue......

Thank you. I'm so sorry… *I chuckle* I'm not one for crying.

No need to apologize. What happen was…

Yes whatever it was, fucking dreadful. *I take another sip of vodka and weep.*

Can I get you anything?

What I need, what I want can't come from you.

As I swallow my next sip of pure vodka my stomach sends a delayed message to my brain... You're over your allotted amount. Please decrease capacity. I immediately jump up and dodge for the bathroom. Oh God, I begin hurling over and over again. When I lift my head from the toilet bowl, behind me standing is Detective Walker with a wet towel in hand.

Don't try to get up, just sit for a moment.
Detective Walker takes the hand towel and places it around my neck.

Through tears and now laughing, I'm so embarrassed could you come back tomorrow? I really need to be alone right now.

Yes I can come back tomorrow but being alone, I don't think it is a good idea. Let me help you up.

I got it *I raise myself up and the floor shifts. I'm back on my ass.*

Let me help you

No I got it!

Damn, you are one stubborn woman. Let me help you, please!

Did this fucking man just say I was stubborn? Did he just yell at me? I burst out with a high pitch laugh.

So now I'm funny. Please put your arm around my neck.

I do as he says and I'm carried over to the couch. Okay I'm fine now. You can be on your way.

Can I get you anything before I go?

I already confirmed I am fine.

Well here's my card. If you need anything *he writes his cell number on the back,* call me… anytime.

Thank you but I won't need anything more, I'm good.

Just in case you do, please do not hesitate to call.

Thank you.

Detective walker walks to the door and exit, closing the door behind him. What am I going to do now? Another drink? Nah I better not. I'll just lay here for a few minutes.

Chapter 5
You Again

My nap lasted more than a few minutes but rather several hours. Already 7:30 in the evening. I'm awaken by a tap at the door.

Who is it?

Ah Detective Walker

What is wrong with this man? Did he not just leave? Opening the door You again?

Yes me again!

How in God's name can I help you now? *Take an easy Beth.*

Well I assumed you were still on your liquid diet and thought maybe you could use something to coat your stomach.

Oh Detective Walker you have jokes.

Yes I guess for a jelly doughnut eating

Oh, Yeah Sorry

No, no I'm sure you meant it.

I do or umm did but

Totally ignoring what I just said, So I brought you Chinese, wonton soup?

Not right now

Just a little *Detective Walker steps into the*

apartment and heads straight to the kitchen. Where are your bowls?

Above the sink

After a few seconds in the kitchen Detective Walker returns to the living-room with a bowl of the soup.

Thanks, what about you?

No I had a large lunch.

Ah, you're not eating and a stranger so… I think maybe I should pass.

Hey, a stranger with a gun who was left alone in your apartment last night when someone, not mentioning any names, but that someone passing out!

You do have a point *we both smile*

Did you get any sleep?

Yes I did, thank you. I know you have better things to do rather than sitting here with me, a family to get home to?

No I'm good *as his lips give away to a partial smile.*

So, umm *with grief and hesitation covering my face, a*ny news on Rosa, you know.

Yes I do and no we are actively working on the case.

I put down my bowl of soup and in an instant pickup Mr. Absolute.

Mrs. Morris you do know you are defeating the purpose of the soup.

With wet eyes, I know *holding back a weep* but good ole Mr. Absolute is becoming a good comforter. *I bring the glass back towards my lips and in an instant Detective Walker is at my side, pulling the glass away. With him being so close I breathe in his scent. Oh he smells soo good.*

Looking me directly in my eyes, You need to find a better way to deal with this.

I chuckle.... If I had other coping mechanisms, I would be practicing them. *I take another sip.*

Well then maybe you should begin researching or better yet talking to someone instead of vodka.

Trying not to go Rambo on this man, I politely smile and purposely pickup Mr. Absolute, pour a rather large shot and in one gulp all gone.

Staring intensely at me... Why do I get the impression you did that to make a point?

Not exactly, I had a thirst and I took care of it.

Wow… Okay I do think it is time for me to go.

Well thank you for the soup, it was really thoughtful.

You are welcome. Ahem… and please do not hesitate to call if…

Thank you but I am good. *I walk to the door and hold it open*

Have a good night Mrs. Morris

You too *and I close the door. With Detective Walker gone I am once again alone and feeling just that. The only way for me to deal is engaging further in my solo pity party with a damn good comforter, my Mr. Absolute.*

You can do this, you can. Oh heavenly father help me through this. Get out the car... Stay strong, get out the car... If I stand right now my legs will buckle. Oh God please get me through this... I beg you.

I make my way into the church, so many people. I'll just take a seat here in the back.

Good Morning, *an usher greets me*

Good Morning

Are you a family member?

No *ahem* friend of the family. Excuse me. *I immediately take a seat in the last row. The church is practically full. I will stay here, in the back. No need to go to the front. Right here is just fine.*

Would everyone please stand for prayer!

The minister begins. I hear his words but all I can do is plead internally. Heavenly father please, please help me get through this.

Please remain standing

As the family comes in I remind myself to stay strong. I close my eyes, my legs are shaking. Please help me through this. While silently asking God for help, for strength I hear someone calling my name, then a tap on the shoulder.

Mrs. Morris, Beth...

I turn to face Jasmine

Beth, please sit with me? Please!

Hi Jasmine *in a whisper* I don't want to take room from your family, I don't want to impose *I can't bare to sit so close.*

Please Beth I know Rosa and Rosie would want this. *Suddenly Jasmine's voice cracks and tears begin to form...* Beth you are family to Rosa, she would never forgive me if...

Interrupting Jasmine I would be honored *and before I could complete my thought I am whisked into the processional alongside Jasmine.*

Walking, Jasmine whispers I tried to call you a few times. It would really mean a lot if you could say a few words.

Jasmine I didn't come prepared.

I know this is short notice but for Rosa, please!

Trying to find the words to say no, I'm guided to the first row of pews, just in front of the two caskets. I keep reminding myself not to look up, to keep my head down. In the midst of my denial, Jasmine taps me on the shoulder once more and whispers This was found in the apartment, the police dropped it off yesterday. It is written out to you.

I examine the envelope - To: Beth Morris. Under, a small traced hand with Rosie's name written in. Overwhelmed I put the envelope in my purse. I resume my avoidance and was able to not acknowledge what is blatantly right in front of me for at least fifteen minutes until...

Next we have a friend of the family to say a few words, Beth Morris.

I stand and try to plan a route around each casket. If I glance at either I will not be able to get through this. I take the longest route to the pulpit, up and around the choir. I know everyone is wondering what I am doing but I don't care.

Finally arriving to the appropriate standing place, I lower my head and close my eyes. Unaware of my loud thoughts I begin to pray. Heavenly father so many times I have called on you. Many times answered other times I felt I was being tested but this time father please get me through this. For Rosa and Rosie please! Daddy, my guardian angel I beg you to give me strength, I beg you.

I lift my head, open my eyes and wipe the tears that manage to escape. Behind me I feel a pat on my shoulder, it is the pastor. He hands me a few tissues and whispers in my ear "Our heavenly father heard your prayer. You have the strength to get through this". *Then loudly says* Amen Church. *Any other time I would find some type of humor in this but this time, this moment I only feel pain and sorrow.*

I've had the honor to know Rosa and Rosie. *keep your head down.... come on...* Anyone who knew Rosa will agree that stubborn and determined are two words that best describes her. *That is right someone yells, others nodding in agreement and a few chuckles.* Stubborn in the sense that whatever the situation, it would be done her way or no way at all. Determined, well whatever she set her mind to, regardless how far fetch it was, whatever the idea Rosa was going to make it happen. And if any decision was going to be made regarding her baby girl *my voice cracks* be ready for the storm because only she would be making that decision. But let me be clear, it wouldn't be a spur of the moment decision. It would be a well thought out - I've done my research and you better have your written proof of how it can be done better on hand. *Smiling* First hand, I've been on the receiving end of that storm and let me tell you, not a pretty scene. But just like Mother Nature, when the storm passes and the sun once again shines Rosa embraces you with open arms. I will miss *I begin to weep, stay strong, don't look across. Do not look right in front of you* I will miss my daily call from Rosa. Whether she was giving me updates or just calling to see how I was doing *my voice strained by my held back tears* I will miss my colored pages, drawings made for me. I will miss two very special people who have *ahem* who has shown me obstacles in life are what you make them. If not acknowledge as an obstacle but rather a goal to conquer you will be living life. Thank you.

Walking back to my seat the choir begins to sing We've Only Just Begun. I force myself to face what I tried to avoid since arriving. I walk to each open casket. Rosa, ever so beautiful I touch her hair, I rub her hand. I will miss you. And my Little Rosie, dressed in her white party graduation dress. On her wrist the bracelet I had given her. I bend and kiss my little Rosie. I whisper to her You gave me life, you made me want to live. *Unable to control my emotions any longer I walk back to the pew pick up my purse and exit the building. I can no longer avoid and can no longer suppress my emotions, I'm about to explode.*

Walking as fast as I can without running, I make it to the top stair outside the church. I find a corner and begin my weeping cry. I begin to question God, questioning how and why he would take either of them but especially a baby who hasn't even begun to live. I question why once again he took someone from me, Just why. Pulling myself together I head for my car. Walking I hear voices. I hear someone confirming who I am, I hear someone questioning why the bitch is at his daughter's funeral. Quicker than my legs would allow I turn on my heel, walk right to Hector's face and dared him to call me a bitch again. Ha! The calm occurred in the church and the storm was about to hit land as a category five hurricane.

Excuse me? Excuse me?

You best back down

Are you fucking talking to me? Hello..?

Listen I advise you to get your stuck-up ass from my face or you will be picking yourself up off the ground.

No this little fuck didn't I wouldn't expect anything different from a woman beater or beg my pardon, a pregnant woman beater. So before you go around calling women bitches so freely maybe just maybe you should pay a visit to your own mother because any woman that carried and delivered your bastard ass must be the biggest bitch of all.

As the last words come out my mouth, in slow motion I see an arm raised. On the end of that arm a hand that comes into direct contact with my left cheek, the force so hard I fall to the ground. As I begin to pick myself up, I see a large foot heading in my direction. I brace myself for the blow but instead I hear a familiar voice.

"I don't think you want to do that".

Detective Walker extends a hand to help me up. In his other hand his gun is drawn and pointed directly at Hector. Are you ok?

I'm fine.

He takes out his cell phone. This is Detective Walker I'm at Christ Deliverance Church between Pitkin and Mother Gaston Boulevard. Send a car… Assault. *Detective Walker turns to Hector.* Turn around and put your hands behind your head.

Yo man you can't be serious my baby girl is dead in that church. You're really going to do this?

Sorry for your loss but that doesn't excuse you from assaulting someone, especially a woman.

Let him go *I say in a whisper.*

Ignored, Detective Walker continues with Hector.

Let him go, leave him alone *I say raising my voice. In disbelief, Detective Walker looks at me.*

Just let him go.

Walking away I hear Detective Walker warning Hector. Fully not understanding what he is telling him but it clearly sounds like a threat.

Mrs. Morris, Mrs. Morris I know you hear me...

Once at my car I turn and respond What?

Are you okay?

I already told you I'm fine. Just let me be.

From what I saw, you're far from fine.

I said I'm fine, so fucking very fine. *I open the car door, get in and pull off as quickly as I can.*

My face feels like it is on fire. What is wrong with me? What am I doing? Not wanting to be alone but needing and wanting a conversation with Mr. Absolute, I set my sights on McFeeny's. Yes I'll have just one drink then head home.

Arriving around noon the bar was preparing itself for all those poor souls like me who needed comfort from a place that doesn't judge. Entering I find that I'm one of the early ones. Other than my arrival just the bartender and two other souls are present. I sit at the end of the bar.

What can I get you?

Straight absolute please

Looking at me with both amusement and disbelief Tough day already?

Yes

Well here you go. Hope this helps.

Within seconds of the bartender putting my shot down is as quickly as I chug it. Can I have another?

Yes I see one bitching of a day. Maybe this one, take it a little slow?

Ahem… Yeah but if you do not mind, can you just leave the bottle?

I guess I could.

By the look on the bartender's face he is unsure if he should engage in conversation with me or not. I guess not since he takes a seat at the opposite end of the bar. That's probably best, as of right this moment I do not think I am able to filter my thoughts.

My drinking continued until the sun is just about to set. Over the course of several hours here I not only finished the bottle of Absolute but I managed to gulp down two gifted shots as well. Barely able to maintain a single thought, I decide to make my way home. Where are my keys? I know I had them. I get off the bar stool to see if I dropped them. My head begins to spin faster and faster. Waving my hands to get the bartender's attention... Excuse me can I have a glass of water?

Sure. Would you like me to call a cab?

No... No *trying not to slur my words.* I'm going to walk.

Are you sure?

Yes, I live nearby. *I take a sip of my water, stand and begin my journey home.*

Walking I'm appreciating the cool summer air hitting my face. Oh but how many more steps. Feeling as if I had been walking for hours I arrive to my apartment about twenty minutes later. I'll just sit here on the step for a few minutes. My head is spinning. I place my head onto my lap. Not even a good minute later I feel someone over me.

Mrs. Morris… Mrs. Morris is this the first time you have been home today?

What? *I look up and in my best drunken Dr. McCoy's voice* "Good God man" *and I burst out laughing.*

Mrs. Morris.... Is this your first time home?

....

Angrily, CAN YOU PLEASE ANSWER THE DAMN QUESTION!

What the fuck is wrong with you *laughing* yes I'm just getting home.

Is someone staying in your apartment?

No *I begin to sing*, no one staying in my apartment – no one staying in my…

Give me your key.

What?

Your key please.

Why????

COULD YOU PLEASE GIVE ME YOUR KEY!

Fumbling I take my keys from my purse. Here *and I toss them to Detective Walker.*

Stay here! Do you hear me? Stay here! *Detective Walker goes into the building*

Tip toe through the valley or is it tulips? Shit tulip… valley… *I begin to laugh.*

Detective Walker returns. He's on his cell phone Send a car over to… home broken into.

What, whose home?

Shh

Oh hell no, did he just shh me? Even louder now... ((Whose Home))??

Detective Walker continues his phone call I'm on the scene.

Whose home was broken into?????

Shh *this time he put his finger over his lips*

Did this fucking man shh me again? ((HELLO))

Ending his call he answers your apartment.

What? *I stand up, stumbling a bit and head to my apartment.*

Let's wait for the police

Wait? (((Hell No))) aren't you the police? *Without any hesitance I run into the building, up the stairs to the second floor, turn right and arrive at apartment 2A right behind me, Detective Walker.*

Do not touch anything.

What the fuck, really? *I can't believe what I see, my home is completely in disarray.*

Do you notice anything missing?

I scan the living room, electronics all in place. I go into my bedroom and all my clothing on the floor. The kitchen, all my food from the refrigerator and freezer tossed all over the place. What the fuck... Why??????

Do you notice anything missing?

Not so far.

Knock… Knock... Knock... Police...

I'm Detective Walker *and he flashes his shield....* So far nothing seems to be missing. No evidence of how the intruder got in. Windows and doors were locked. Start dusting and lift any prints you can.

In disbelief I begin to question why this is happening. Then in the midst of my sudden pity party I realize that I don't see Gizmo. Shit where is he? ((Gizmo))..... ((Gizmo))... (((Gizmo)))…. *Where is he?*

Detective Walker walks over to me Mrs. Morris what is it *a puzzled look on his face*

Gizmo… I don't see him and he hasn't responded to me calling him.

Detective Walker and I begin looking throughout the apartment, looking in all closets, cabinets and storage spaces. No sign of Gizmo.

Officer, *Detective Walker summons* scan out front and the building for a black and white cat. Weighing about 20 pounds, answers to Gizmo.

Unable to sustain my emotions I yell out He wouldn't leave the apartment, he won't even go into the hall.

Realization of Gizmo not answering, I begin to sober up. Taking in the chaos around me, my personal belongs on display for every fucking officer in my apartment right now. Why is this happening? I turn to get some possible answers from Detective Walker but he's off in an animated conversation with another detective? When will this day end?

Approximately forty-five minutes later, my apartment begins to become scarce of the many bodies it was holding.

Detective Walker we searched the building and surrounding areas, no cat.

Alright thanks.

This fucking day! Who would want to do this? For what? The only item missing, my cat?

Mrs. Morris, you should arrange to get your locks changed first thing in the morning.

Yeah, okay *and I exhale.*

Can you stay with a family member this evening?

What? Why*? Not giving time for him to answer* I'm fine right here.

I beg to differ. Call your sister, Cynthia?

Sure, I'll call after everyone leaves.

The last officers are heading out. Detective Walker follows but turns to me "Call your sister".

I will. I'll be out in ten minutes. I just need a moment to myself.

Can I ask you one question before I go?

I guess...

Hector Rodriguez, does he know where you live?

No, I don't think so.

Ever give anything to Rosa with your address or Telephone number?

Rosa has my telephone number and yes both Rosa and Rosie have been to my home many times.

Okay, ten minutes.

Yes I'll be out in ten. Good night!

Call if you need anything.

I close the door behind Detective Walker. Taking in my surroundings I attempt to clean up, beginning in the kitchen, what a mess. Food taken out of the refrigerator, tossed on the floor why? I go to take cleaning supplies from under the sink and notice Gizmo's food is missing? I turn to scan his dish, gone? I check my bedroom for his scratching post hut. Gone too? This isn't making any sense. Someone took my cat? Why? Must be a reason? Cynthia is the only one with a key. But she wouldn't just come over, take Gizmo? I pick up the phone and call.

Hey Cynthia

Hi Beth… Weren’t you supposed to call me back a few days ago?

Sorry, been a little busy. How are you?

Don't try to change the subject.

I'm not

So what is wrong?

Just wanted to know if you came by my place today?

No.... why?

No reason. Oh sorry Cynthia my cell is ringing, I will call you back. *A little white lie and before I give her the opportunity to call me a liar I hang up. What the hell is going on? I pour myself a little of Mr. Absolute to help me understand what is going on. The phone rings.*

I didn't mean to hang up so quickly *another lie*

Hello?

Oh fucking bloody hell, yes Detective Walker?

Just checking to see if you left already?

Yup I did. I’m walking to my car now.

Really?

Yes. So thank you and I will talk to you another time, Good night! *I hang up the phone. Startled by two loud knocks on my door, I jump.*

Who is it?

Detective Walker

You're fucking kidding me. Is this a joke? I swing open the door.

Wow, amazing you made it from your car that quickly. By the way do you even know where your car is?

Holy shit, I forgot I parked by McFeeney's. You found me out. Listen I'm fine, no worries so please go tend after someone that needs tending to.

Mrs. Morris, I really don't think you take this matter seriously. Your apartment was broken into and the only item that seems to be missing is your cat and all his items.

How do you know his items are missing?

I noticed and by the way you answered the phone you were not honest with your sister regarding what occurred here this evening!

Listen it's been a very long and exhausting day, all I want to do is go to bed so on that note, good night Detective Walker!

You're absolutely correct, you did have an eventful exhausting day so please grab your purse and come with me.

What?

Listen you can't sleep here tonight, not until the locks have been changed.

I can!

You can't and you won't. We can do this the hard way or my way?

Your delusional right now aren't you?

Please get your purse.

Listen it is late and my family is all the way on the other side of Queens. I'm fine right here Detective Walker.

Well I live in the building where you forgot… ahem… left your car.

He lives that close? Great to hear you live nearby but I can't stay in your apt. Do we need to review the whole stranger thing?

Do we need to review I have a gun and stayed in an apartment with a woman who barely could spell her name due to her solo party with a Mr. Absolute?

Instantly I burst out laughing, you won this round. *I pick up my purse and walk out the door. I sit quietly during the ride to his home. When we arrive, I check on my car and follow Detective Walker to his third floor apartment.*

Please come in.

Detective Walker leads me into a modernized decorated apartment. African and Asian art displayed, wall to wall bookcases filled, and artwork on the walls. Stairs leading to a loft area houses exotic plants on each step. Along the length of the kitchen and dining room, French doors that lead to a large terrace that overlooks the Throgs Neck Bridge. But oddly, no personal photos nor objects that would personalize one's home.

You have a beautiful apartment.

Thank you.

Can I get you anything? And please do not ask for Mr. Absolute.

No... No thank you.

Well, you can take my room here. *He leads me into a large master suite. Again picture perfect but lacks personalization*

The bed has fresh sheets.

No, I can't put you out any further, the couch is just fine.

You're not putting me out. Very rarely do I sleep in my bed I'm more of a couch guy.

Ok well thank you and good night.

Mrs. Morris, ah here... *he pulls out a large tee shirt* and if you want, sweat pants or shorts. I promise all clean.

Ha on a different day that would have been my question and please call me Beth.

Oh... okay Beth, and through that door you will find the bathroom. Fresh towels top shelf.

With a smile thank you.

Chapter 6
Taunting Emotions

I sit on the bed and begin undressing. I don't want to think about this day any further, I just want to sleep. I search my purse for a hair tie but instead I find the envelope given to me earlier by Jasmine. I forgot I had it. Should I read it now or should I wait? I'll read it now and get it over with. I change into Detective Walker's tee shirt, walk to the end of the bed and sit on the floor. I begin to review the envelope. To Beth and under, a traced picture of Rosie's hand. My eyes begin to swell. Maybe this isn't a good time to do this. I continue inspecting the envelope. Inside consist of a thank you card and a two page letter. I begin to read the thank you card. The cover... Thank you.... Inside ... Thank you for being who you are, love Rosa and Rosie.....a smile emerges. I begin to unfold and read the letter.

The Letter

Dearest Beth:

With both sadness and relief I write this letter. I know for the past few months I've given you the impression that my health has been fine, often even over exaggerating but the truth is just the opposite. It has come to the time to put my affairs in order and I need to start with my one prized possession, my little girl.

Since Rosie's birth, I can only recall one consistent person in our lives and that person being you Beth Morris. For every birthday, holiday and even made up holidays you have been with us. You are always the first person at my door when either Rosie or I are ill. You have always been with us in our time of need and Rosie and I are ever so grateful. You gave Rosie and me life, something to look forward to, something to hope for. The few times I allowed myself to feel pity and dwell on what will not be, you always brought me back to the here and now, reinforcing the blessing I have and reminding me that tomorrow isn't promised to anyone. If Rosie and I didn't have you in our lives I would have given up a long time ago and would not have had the opportunity to experience life with my little girl, the little girl I am asking you to take in and raise as your own.

Beth I know this is a big imposition but when I look at the supports in my life and the people I completely trust, my list is very small with you at the top. I hope you will accept this request because I know Rosie is going to need you and ironically I think you need her as well. Since Rosie's birth, you and she has had a bond that I initially didn't understand and maybe still don't but one thing is for sure, I am grateful for that bond because when my time comes I can rest in peace knowing that my little girl is with someone who loves her as much as her mother.

Elizabeth Morris, before I end I do have one other request. This New Year's Eve and all others, please ring it in with Rosie. Of all the holidays this is the only time Rosie and I don't see you and at 12:00 a.m. on January 1st when I call you, I hear such sadness in your voice. So a new tradition to

begin this year! If I'm around, the three of us will celebrate like no other New Year's celebration, like it is the last. If just you and Rosie, promise me the same. Celebrate with joy and absolutely no mourning for me because if not in person I will be with both of you in spirit. So, from "it's you and me kid" to you and my baby girl, we love you Beth.....
Always Rosa and Rosie

Finishing the letter my weeping becomes uncontrollable. Where do I go from here? This emptiness, I feel so alone. Oh God how could you do this to me. Why? Will I ever feel this love again?

Tap... Tap...

Mrs. Morris, Beth... are you okay?

....

Beth?

Tears falling I'm fine.... sorry to wake you.

I'm coming in.

Detective Walker enters the room and sits by me on the floor. He puts his arms around me. The physical affection heavies my heart and I can't control my tears.

Beth, what can I do or say, how can I make this better for you?

Raising the letter Bring them back to me.

Holding me tighter, I wish I could.

Why would anyone want to do this? Why?

Caressing my arm I don't know but we will find out, I promise.

Don't make promises that are out of your control.

I don't!

Please, get some rest, I'm fine.

I'm comfortable right here.

After a few minutes of silence I begin to laugh. The other evening, ah… did I say or do anything that I should apologize for?

Blushing Not really, frequently I'm asked if I prefer boxers or briefs.

I'm so embarrassed and very sorry.

No… no I have to say, you were quite entertaining. But since we are on this subject can I ask you a question?

Detective Walker… *Interrupted*

Kevin please

With a smile Kevin, since meeting you when haven't you not asked me a question?

True. *His lips sporting a smile* But this one is very important. Did I see an Elvis collection?

Ha... Yes you did. Why?

I don't know too many young black women with an Elvis Presley collection. Better yet, black people in general.

Well, let me introduce myself. My name is Elizabeth Morris, I am of Creole descent via Shreveport Louisiana and I love, love, love Elvis Aaron Presley.

A black woman who loves Elvis? Wow, this is a first for me.

I'm not the only black woman with this fetish. My grandmother was an even bigger fan. I remember growing up, every Sunday on channel five she and I would watch Elvis movies.

Really? *Detective Walker looking amused.*

Why do I get the sense your dying laughing inside?

Sporting a large smile No I'm just amazed.

Well what else did you notice in my apartment? *All of a sudden a frightening thought. With a horrified look on my face,* did you see anything else?

Like what?

Anything… *Feeling a bit relieved.*

I didn't see any personal items displayed on the floor. Oh crap I forgot to pick up bullets for my gun.

Oh how embarrassing. I bury my head into my lap. He saw my unmentionable.

Laughing..... What, I just said I had...

Please don't say it again... *We both laugh.*

A few days ago you inquired if I was generous

Interrupted, I'm really sorry for that.

Please, don't be because now I'm posing the same question. Do you show this level of concern for all the cases you are solving?

With compassion in his voice No I don't.

Not sure how to feel about his response, then why? Why me?

Because you are you!

What does that mean?

I didn't understand the relationship between Rosa Morales and you until talking with your supervisor, who by the way spoke very highly of you. Then the letter Ms. Morales wrote you.

This letter? *With a bit of anger in my voice,* You read it?

Yes, going through the items found in the home, I read the letter and thought you should have it. I brought it back to Ms. Morale's sister a few days ago.

Clutching the letter close to my heart and tears trickling down my face... Thank you. Receiving this letter gives me a little bit of life back.

You are very welcomed.

Touching my left cheek and looking me directly in the eyes, so to answer your original question no I do not show this level of care. You are the first. I just wish you would take what is going on seriously.

I do... It's just that... I do. Rosa and Rosie were very special to me.

I get that. It isn't everyday someone hands over their child.

Lifting himself up onto his feet, Kevin extends his hand. I place mine into his and swiftly I am swept onto my feet. Kevin leaves the room and I climb into bed. He returns with a frozen bag of peas.

Your face is beginning to swell. Hold this against your face.

Thank you.

As he removes his hand from my face, Kevin lifts my chin. Do you know you have amazing eyes, one lighter than the other?

What really? Oh my goodness *I say jokingly and blushing.* Thank you. Well Kevin it has been a very long day and I don't want to keep you any longer.

Good night Beth. If you need anything I'm right on the couch.

Thank you.

Closing the door behind him, I climb into bed. So many emotions and uncertainties. The one thing I'm sure about, I don't want to be alone. My first instinct is to ask Kevin to sit with me but I really don't want to give him the wrong impression. Who am I trying to fool? Yes I am attracted to him. Yes he makes me smile. So what's the problem? The problem is I don't do relationships. No we don't connect that way and with good reason. But I don't want to be alone and I shouldn't be? Taking the lead from my inner voice I get out of bed, grab a pillow and walk to the living room. Upon entering Kevin is laying on the couch reading a book with the sounds of Gladys Knight playing softly in the background, Midnight Train to Georgia.

Kevin I don't want to be alone, do you mind if I sit out here with you for a bit?

Extending his hand, Kevin leads me to sit beside him. Once seated he takes his arm and wraps it around me

Is this better?

More than you would ever know.... Yes it is.

As he continues to read I begin to fall asleep finally putting today's events to rest at least for the moment.

Waking up to my cell phone ringing, I jump up forgetting where I am. Looking around I set sight onto Detective Kevin Walker. Tall, clean shaven, caramel tone and ever so fine of a man.

Ring… Ring

Who is calling me at this time? Trying not to wake Kevin I untangle myself from his comforting hold.

Ring… Ring

I head into the bedroom where my cell phone is

Hello?

Beth I'm sorry to call you so early. I tried your apartment but no answer.

Mrs. Frankel. What's wrong?

Sweetie I don't know how to tell you this but I was out walking Franklin and... Oh sweetie, I found

Gizmo on the back side of the building, Honey he is no longer with us.

(((What))))

Sorry Beth

Why is this happening? I'll be home in ten minutes.

I'll wait for you Beth.

Hanging up, I throw my hands to my face.

What happen? *Kevin standing in the doorway*

Tears filling my eyes, my neighbor found Gizmo. She found him on the side of the building. *I begin to sob*

Give me two minutes and I'll come with you.

Kevin thanks but no thank you. I'm fine. You've done so much already. *Not realizing I was getting dressed in front of Kevin, I take off Kevin's shirt and put back on my clothes, all done in less than five minutes.*

I'm coming with you... nothing more to be said.

Ten minutes later I'm back at my apartment. Mrs. Frankel waiting by the front door as promised.

Sweetie I put him here in the box.

Taking the box from Mrs. Frankel I begin to cry.

Awe honey I'm so sorry *Mrs. Frankel's tone changes right around the moment Kevin put his arm around me then an alarmed look.* Beth what happened to your face? *Her tone of both care and concern.*

Long story Mrs. Frankel, but I'm ok.

Beth let me take the box *Kevin attempts to take the box from my hands.*

No I have it. I just want to spend a little time with him.

Mrs. Frankel leans over to Kevin and whispers Beth has had him since the first day she moved in, that was almost ten years ago. Gizmo was a gift from her dad and he passed away a few years ago.

Mrs. Frankel where did you say you found him?

I don't mean to be rude but you are?

This is Detective Walker.

Detective huh…

Yes Mrs. Frankel.

I'll walk you over..... *Mrs. Frankel says with a complex look.*

Beth, please wait here. We will go into the apartment together, okay?

Beth are you in some type of trouble? What is going on? *Mrs. Frankel looking genuinely concerned.*

No Mrs. Frankel. No worries. *I then look at Kevin* Sure.... *answering his question. I sit on the stoop waiting for Kevin to return.*

Approximately five minutes later Kevin returns. Beth I need to have Gizmo checked.

Checked? What do you mean checked?

I would like the medical examiner to take a look at him?

Are you kidding me? *Tears streaming*

Sorry but I must.

Taking my hand into his Kevin leads us into my apartment building. As much as I want to pull away I find myself grasping his hand tighter. Unlocking my door, Gizmo's death hits. when I open this door Gizmo won't be in his marked spot, sitting as if he stayed in the same position all day, not moving until I was back home. Having Gizmo gave me the feeling that daddy was around, looking over me. Providing me with strength on the days I felt I didn't have any. The feeling hits hard.

Oh come on, don't cry *Kevin says with compassion in his voice.*

I open the door and step in. It is final, my house no longer my home. My house is just a place now to lay my head.

Chapter 7
One's Life in a Box

I never realized how much stuff I've collected over the years. But realization hits when I see my life spread out across my apartment. From room to room I take in property meant to be viewed by some and other things to be seen by one... me. I don't understand the intrusion and certainly do not understand the timing. Could Hector have done this? Is he responsible for killing two of the most important people in my life? Why? Why now? And Gizmo, to break into my home, trash it, take my cat and all his items? I feel as if I'm losing control. A feeling I haven't felt in some time. Feelings that once took me to a very dark place, a place I promised to never travel to again. But the odds are stacking up against me right now. I don't like the place I'm in and only I - me can get me out of it.

Finally on the last room destroyed by who? I begin sorting through clothing on the floor. Folding all, I then pick up my un-mentionable that is sitting in plain sight. With embarrassment written across my face I immediately pickup my little friend and place it back into my night stand drawer. Now to tackle my closet! Shit whomever did this hit every niche of my home. I pick up my photo albums that were hidden away in the back of my closet. Turning the pages I'm brought back to my wedding, the joke of the decade. Pictures of Michael and me, him in his Army dress blues and me in this outrageous fairytale ball gown. Keyword -fairytale! Ha, unfortunately that day was the last day of my happiness.

Looking through the albums I notice pictures missing, leaving only open space on pages. Trying to recall if at some point in my fit of anger, destroyed them? Ha, knowing the place I was in I probably did. But wow, it took all these years to notice. Well nothing you can do about it now I tell myself. Besides, the reason why I had the damn books hidden was to dismiss that time of my life.

I continue cleaning until the last speck of my home invasion was masked by my cleanup. From the outside order has been restored, material objects are back to their rightful place and necessities that haven't been contaminated by another's touch stored. Yes I accomplished a lot since seven this morning but for my heart and my soul emptiness is my only fulfillment. As I sit here in this fully furnished empty apartment, my thoughts run rampant. Trying with great difficulty not to question you heavenly father, but a difficult task. I'm trying to understand why at one point in my life I was spared when I begged not to be. Such a cruel joke. Now you allow me to live but yet others around me who gave me a reason to be thankful for another day taken away. Why? I only ask for a sign heavenly father, a sign to show me I can be loved and give love, all unconditional. Ending my rant to God, someone is at my door.

Knock… Knock

Who is it?

Beth it is me, Kevin.

Take the smile off your face Beth. This cannot happen and it won't. I open the door and Detective Walker with his ever so handsome self is standing in front of me with a large box in hand.

Good evening Detective Walker

I thought we were passed all the formalities?

With a smile and what gave you that impression Detective Walker? But please come in.

Wow you really got this place back together in a few hours.

Yes I did. Please have a seat. So what questions did you come to ask this evening? *Smiling at Kevin*

Well this evening I am question less *he says with a chuckle*. I came by to see how you were and to give you this *Kevin hands me the box.*

What is it?

Open it…

I sit the box on the coffee table and proceed to the kitchen. Can I get you anything?

If not too much trouble can I have a glass of water?

I can do one better, instead of tap, w*alking from the refrigerator* here's a nice cold bottle of water.

Thank you.

As Kevin sips his water I hear a scratching sound coming from the box.

Ah Kevin what's in the box?

I suggest you open it to find out

With hesitance I walk over to the box and take off the lid. Oh my goodness, he or she is very beautiful. But Kevin why are you walking around with a kitten in a box?

I'm not walking around with him in a box *said with a smirk.* I thought maybe you could use a friend and this little guy needs a family.

My eyes glossy from held back tears, I take the kitten out of the box and rub my nose against his. Thank you so much Kevin, this was ever so thoughtful.

You're welcome *Kevin stands and walks toward the door.*

Are you leaving already?

Yes but I also have this for you *on the outside of my apartment door Kevin drags in two large bags.* This should be everything you need for this guy.

Looking through the bags I remove the items Cat litter, litter box, food and dishes. This is very kind of you…. Thank you.

You are welcomed. Okay I will be on my way.

Really, you're leaving already?

With a smirk, I didn't want to over stay my welcome.

Well the kitten gained you a few brownie points so if you want I can order a pizza? My treat!

I would love that.

While Kevin and I wait for the pizza to be delivered, I begin to ask questions about Rosa and Rosie's case. Do you know yet who umm, who harmed Rosie and Rosa?

No not yet.

Can you tell me if you have any leads?

No, no leads.

Why do I get the impression that any question I ask will not be answered?

No I will answer the ones not associated with the case *said with a smile.* Beth during your cleanup did you note any missing items?

No, unfortunately.

Unfortunately? *Kevin says with a puzzled look.*

Yes, Maybe if the television, stereo and even jewelry… Wait a second *I immediately jump up and head to my bedroom. Looking through my jewelry box I search for my wedding set. This is odd. I always keep it here. I begin looking on the floor to see if I overlooked the rings while cleaning. As I'm on all fours Kevin stands in the doorway.*

Beth what are you looking for?

My wedding set. I kept it in that jewelry box and when cleaning I don't recall seeing it.

Kevin steps into the room and begin looking as well. When was the last time you saw it?

It isn't something I look at daily. I guess a few months back.

Ah Beth what is the status of your marriage?

I look up at Kevin who seems to have a complex look... I've been divorced for several years.

Do you maintain contact with your ex-husband?

Don't you think that is an odd question?

No, actually I don't think it is.

No I do not maintain contact with him. Besides he resides somewhere in the south. Now let me ask you a few questions.

Sounding hesitant Sure

Are you currently or have been married?

No I've never been married and I don't have any children. Any other questions?

No, no further questions. *Once confirming I had no further questions my buzzer rings.*

I'll get it *and Kevin heads for the door.*

I go into the kitchen for my purse. By the time I get to the door Kevin already paid and began setting the table.

Please tell me you didn't pay for the pizza, this was on me!

Beth no worries!

Sounding a bit annoyed Thank you. What can I get you to drink?

Anything non-alcohol Beth

How about Pepsi?

Perfect

Kevin and I sit and eat. I love the company, the presence of another... who am I kidding, the presence of Kevin... feels good. While eating Kevin inquires about my wedding ring.

Beth do you have any pictures?

Puzzled by the question I should but why?

The rings need to be reported as missing. If a picture exists, local pawn shops could be searched.

I walk into the bedroom and pull out the same albums I just put away earlier. As I'm looking through the albums Kevin who follows me into my bedroom questions the empty spaces.

Why do you have empty spaces?

I questioned that myself earlier today, when cleaning up. Probably something I did.

Did how?

Who knows, I haven't looked at any of this in years, not until today. Whoever broke in left no stone unturned!

Beth stop touching the book..... Leave it.

As Kevin directs me to not touch the albums, he pulls out his cellphone Ericsson, Walker, I'm at the Morris residence. Can you swing by, we may have something… Okay see you in a few.

Can I ask why this person is coming by?

To see if we can lift any prints off the albums as well as the jewelry box. Beth why didn't you tell me about this earlier?

Huh?

Hello?

Kevin I didn't think it was anything and it very well be just that, nothing.

Listen, within a short amount of time several things occurred all of which effects / affected you. Up to a few minutes ago we had nothing to go by.

Kevin I don’t know. Maybe all that occurred is one big coincidence.

Beth your cat and all his items missing? A family that you were very close to... So close the mother wanted you to become the legal guardian of her daughter, both murdered? Too many coincidences Beth! You really don't take any of this seriously do you?

Chapter 8
No Stone Unturned

By the time Kevin was done outlining my neglect, Detective Ericsson and two uniformed officers are at my door.

Erickson... Thanks for coming by. *Kevin leads Detective Erickson and the two uniformed officers to my bedroom. Sitting and waiting for the officers to finish, my unnamed kitty and I fall asleep on the couch. Awaken approximately forty-five minutes later by the closing of my door.*

Hey how long have I been asleep?

Just a few minutes

Oh *I begin to get up, Kevin blocking my move*

Where are you going?

I can only imagine the mess left in my bedroom.

No mess I promise. No need to get up the rest will do you some good.

No I'm ok. By the way, were they able to get any clues?

We will know in a few hours.

Glancing at the clock on my stereo, 10:00 p.m. wow... I'm sure you need to get going.

No not in any rush, unless I'm overstaying my welcome?

No, not at all *I say with a chuckle* I feel I've monopolized a great deal of your time.

Well I do not feel that way and if you don't mind, I would like to stay here tonight.

Stay here???

On the couch! I'm beginning to sense someone has a filthy mind.

Ha ... No..... but I would like that.

I have a change of clothing in my gym bag. I'll run down to my car and grab my bag.

As Kevin leaves the apartment I begin to question what I'm doing. You cannot and will not fall for this man. Too much is going on right now and no way can I revert from what is going on around me. Can it be that Michael is doing this? But why? No it can't be. I haven't spoken to him in almost ten years. Besides, what happen, what I did affected him from what I've been told? But once a sick bastard always a sick bastard? No, there has to be some other explanation and I need to dig a bit further to understand what is going on around me. More importantly, why would anyone brutally murder two people that... None of this makes any since. Ending my venting session with self, Kevin returns with a small black gym bag and a rather large book.

Beth would it be okay to shower?

Oh good God yes... Sure, I'll get you what you need. *Walking toward the bathroom I can't help but notice how tight this man's body is. No! No! No! Beth, we don't do relationships especially right now. Shut it down.*

I left what you need on the sink. I'll also get my bed ready for you. I mean you will sleep in my room. *Oh my God!!!*

Blushing, No the couch is fine. I told you before I'm kind of a couch sleeper.

Well whatever your pleasure

.... Awkward silence

With a smirk, Ah I'm going to take that shower now.

With a smile back I head to my bedroom.

About 30 minutes later Kevin is standing in my bedroom doorway wearing a pair of NBA Bulls shorts and a white tank. This man looks absolutely delicious. Excuse me Beth, wondering if you wanted to watch a movie or something on TV?

Wow is this one of your typical Saturday nights? *I say with a chuckle.*

Nothing wrong with staying in on a Saturday evening especially if you're spending it with someone you enjoy being around.

Well I'm sure I'm not your first choice, but sure.

My only choice, meet you in the living room.

I grab my pillow and blanket and go to living room. I sit on the floor with my back against the couch.

Do you mind if I join you down there?

I'm sure I can make room *I say with a smile.*

As Kevin goes through the channels, my eyes take notice of a picture sitting on the lower shelf of my coffee table. I pick it up and scan the photo from this past Cinco de Mayo. Yes Rosa was correct, I celebrated any and every holiday, always with Rosie and Rosa and this photo taken of Rosie and me by Rosa tells the story. All three of us dressed in extra-large sombreros and ponchos. A party just to celebrate! Since Rosie's birth, Cinco de Mayo has been celebrated between the three of us. I remember the first year... Rosie was only a few months old. I arrived to Rosa's with sombreros, ponchos and a cake. Rosa thought I was absolutely nuts but year after year the party got bigger and bigger... Wow May 5th will now be just that, May 5th!

Tears begin to form and fall. Not sure how many times Kevin called my name but he caught my attention as his hand wipes away my tears.

Beth are you okay?

Oh yes, just a silly memory, *I say as I stand and head into the kitchen.* Can I get you a drink?

No Beth, I'm not a drinker.

Okay, *I pour myself a shot and gulp it down. I pour another and return to my seat on the floor.*

Beth....you need to talk to someone about this.

Thrown by the statement, anger surfaces... EXCUSE ME?

Not trying to piss you off, just an observation. You're not doing okay and drinking your memories away, you're hurt? How is that working for you?

Trying not to explode, I change the subject... So did you find anything?

With an annoyed expression No I haven't.

After a few minutes of silence, I suggest we watch TV Land. A Dick Van Dyke Marathon is on. Do you want to watch?

Sure.... Are you a fan?

Ha, I'm afraid to answer after the Elvis thing.

With a chuckle, I'll give you a pass on this. I'm a fan of old shows Green Acres, Mr. Ed, The Ghost and Mrs. Mur etc.

So am I *we both laugh.*

As time passes I find myself napping a little. Squirming to make myself comfortable Kevin in a low tone suggest that I get into bed and not worry about him.

Thanks Kevin but I rather not be alone. During the day I'm okay but when night falls...

Well I'm here tonight. *Kevin takes the pillow I had behind me and places it across his lap. With my new unnamed kitty in my arms I lay my head down. Trying to think of only happy thoughts I fall asleep.*

Approximately around 3am I'm awakened by the sudden movement of Kevin getting up.

What's wrong?

Not sure… I'll be right back.

Huh?

Please this one time stay put! I'll be right back. *Kevin slips on his shoes, takes his gun out and leaves the apartment.*

What the hell. What did I miss? I walk toward voices in the hallway. Mrs. Frankel? I rush out my apartment and approach Mrs. Frankel.

What's going on?

Beth someone kept ringing my buzzer. Sounded like a woman. She said she was your sister and she was concerned about you. She requested that I let her in and I did.

My sister? Mrs. Frankel Cynthia has a key to my home.

I didn't have a good feeling about it so I decided to walk down to your apartment to check on you. When I opened my door and looked down the hallway the person was doing something to your door. I yelled "hey what are you doing" but the person ran....

By the time Mrs. Frankel ended, Kevin was back... I thought I asked you to stay put?

You did but...

Mrs. Frankel are you sure it was a woman? Did you see a face? *Kevin's voice presenting anxious*

No I didn't. I'm so sorry

Mrs. Frankel you did nothing wrong *I say to hopefully make her feel better, not responsible.*

Mrs. Frankel you try to get some rest. I will come by later this morning to see how you are.

You're such a gentleman Kevin. Beth a real gentleman *this time said with a smile.*

Good night Mrs. Frankel *smiling back.*

Kevin what did I miss...*asking as we go back into my apartment.*

I thought I heard someone outside your door, turning the door knob. But within a few seconds of noticing I heard Mrs. Frankel yelling. *Kevin takes out his cell* Erickson sorry for calling so late. I'm at the Morris residence, someone just tried to break in.... No, seems neighbor buzzed person in. Arrange a car to circle residence tonight. Right... Okay see you about seven.

What now? *I ask with attitude.*

Let's just get some rest.

Why do I get the feeling it will be me sleeping and you not?

It is what I do.

Well we can do it together. *I go into the kitchen and make both coffee and tea.* Kevin what do you take in your coffee?

Nothing, black please

Sure *I walk back into the living room and hand Kevin a cup of coffee. I sit on the couch and begin sipping my tea.*

Beth I know you're tired of the questions but right now we need to review why someone is trying to get to you.

I guess it is me huh?

It looks that way. Can you put together a list of clients that you have had difficulties with?

I really haven't had any.

Well what you do come with pissed off husbands, mates. Anyone comes to mind?

Really I've been lucky.

Are you going into work on Monday?

That's my plan. Why?

I need you to put together a list of people you have worked with.

Kevin that really isn't necessary.

Please could you just do it?

I will need to discuss with Rochelle first.

Do what you need to. I will also get the District Attorney's Office involved.

Kevin, I Just don't know how it could be anyone I know personally or even worked with. Plus what would be the connection with Rosa?

Can you tell me about your ex.... Where does he live and when was the last time you saw him?

Kevin now you're really reaching, *needless to say being a bit intrusive* I haven't had contact with him for almost ten years and last I knew he resided in the south.

As Kevin questions begin to lessen I lean back on the couch and close my eyes. Not wanting to re-live my last encounter with Michael my mind drifts back to that exact time and place.

November 25, 1988

Beth I'm Dr. Benningfield can you hear me? Beth?

I hear you but why? Why are you asking me questions? I'm not here anymore.

Mr. Morris your wife lost a lot of blood. She is stable now but unfortunately we could not save the pregnancy.

Pregnancy? What pregnancy?

Your wife was approximately sixteen weeks, second trimester.

……………

She is significantly underweight especially for how far along she was in the pregnancy. When was the last time she saw her Obstetrician?

……………

Was she being followed by an Obstetrician or Gynecologist?

……………

Are you alright Mr. Morris?

What caused her to lose the baby?

Your wife endured significant physical trauma. X-rays show a poorly healed rib fracture seems months old. Can you tell me what happen?

……………

Your wife has several contusions to her arms, legs and a hand print around her neck. How did this happen?

……………

Mr. Morris?

God this is a joke right? Why am I here? Am I to be grateful that I'm returning as one and not as two? Am I to be grateful for that? I feel tears trickling down my face but I can't open my eyes.... I can't speak. How can it be that you heavenly father played this very cruel joke on me. Why?

Mr. Morris, can you tell me what happened?

Michael what happen?

Just when the doctor inquires once more I hear a familiar voice.

What the fuck is going on?

What happen to my baby girl?

Cynthia? Daddy?

Dad... I'm sorry.

Michael crying, Lord you're playing this joke to the fullest.

Beth daddy and I are here.

Cynthia why are you here? No, this isn't how it was to go. I was to come home to you and daddy in a box. Not like this...

Michael come here... Come here now! *I hear deep anger in Cynthia's voice*

What is all this? How did this happen? My father can't see her like this. What happen? *Cynthia not giving Michael a chance to answer*

Cynthia I'm sorry.

Sorry? Sorry?

I hear another voice You must be her father?

Yes I am and her sister Cynthia. What can you tell us?

I hear a pause.....

Do not look at him for approval *Cynthia referring to the doctor looking to Michael for permission.* I want to know right now what the hell is going on. *Cynthia's anger increasing.*

It seems to be attempted suicide. Your sister made... cut both wrist and her inner thigh.

I hear my father gasping

Your sister lost a lot blood but is stable at this time. However we weren't able to save the pregnancy.

Pregnancy *Cynthia yells out*

Yes she was approximately sixteen weeks

Why do I have to hear this again? Once is more than enough!

What about the bruises?

No doubt your sister was assaulted. Detective Harris is working on this case. He is waiting to speak with Mrs. Morris.

Michael what do you know about this? *Cynthia's voice sounding very strained.*

I hear my father's voice cracking... What happen to my baby girl?

Daddy, Beth wouldn't want you to see her like this. Let me take you out to the waiting area.

What did I do? God you weren't supposed to let me see light again. Why? What did I do? I feel tears trickling down my face once again. All I can think of is my dad. What did I do?

Cynthia returns. This time I hear pure anger in her voice Michael what happen?

Cynthia...

What happen!

Cynthia I will never forgive myself.

You did this to her? WHY?

……..........

((WHY))

Cynthia I.... Cynthia I'm so sorry.

Why, why did you? How could you?

I don't know Cynthia I will never forgive myself.

Forgive yourself??? Forgive yourself? You are one sick fucking bastard. You beat her while carrying your child? Beat her in general? Such a real man! *And just as Cynthia begins her rage, I hear another voice*

Do not talk to my son that way.

Bitch you lost your mind didn't you? Don't talk to your son that way? Take a look at my sister. Look at her good and long.

…………

Huh? Tears really? For my sister or for your manly son who if you haven't heard did this knowing she was pregnant... Sixteen weeks pregnant!

I didn't know. I did not know, she didn't tell me.

Would it have made a difference?

As Cynthia continues to question Michael I feel someone rubbing my arm...

Beth my son really loves you.

Let me the fuck up. Bitch, are you kidding me? Loves me? Yes with every smack with every name... Yup he loves me. Someone please get this woman away from me.

Paulette, if you don't mind my father and I would like some time alone with my sister.

This woman better comply. If the anger in Cynthia's voice translates to physical emotion, Paulette will never recover from Cynthia's wrath. So get out and take your fucked up son with you. Oh Cynthia you always know what I need and want.

After a few minutes of silence I smell a familiar scent. Royal Copenhagen, my dad's signature scent. I feel a kiss on my fore head and a hand rubbing the top of my head, my father's signature move. I feel the tears falling down my face.

Beth can you hear me? Beth *this time her voice cracking*. Beth open your eyes.

I try over and over again. I can't open my eyes and I can't speak. Trying Harder, all I can manage are more tears. After several attempts to make any part of my body move I'm internally exhausted. I fall asleep.

Not sure how long I had been asleep, I awake to my dad sleeping in the chair to my left and Cynthia reading a newspaper to my right.

So this is what it takes to get you to the South? *I say in a whisper...*

Beth, Beth, Beth I would have been here much sooner for much, much less. *Cynthia gets up with tears falling and kisses my forehead.* Daddy she's awake.

My baby girl *is all that my father can manage to say. He begins to breakdown.*

Daddy, please don't cry. Please I'm okay.

Beth.... I can't lose you.

With tears streaming down my face I can only manage "I love you daddy"*. But that was only part truth. I loved my dad but staying in darkness trumped my love for my father and anyone else. God played a horrible joke on me.*

About an hour passed and I am faced with giving a full report to a Detective Harris. Allowing Cynthia to stay with me I ask my dad to get me a drink from the cafeteria. I wanted to spare him from any details.

I reviewed the many instances of my beatings, hits, verbal abuse etc. I confirmed that it was I who cut my wrist and inner thigh. I further confirmed Michael's unawareness about the pregnancy. Although Cynthia presented as strong, I saw in her eyes her concern for me. Ending his interview, Detective Harris informs us of the warrant that will be put out for Michael. In the meantime an order of protection would be applied for. He further wanted to know my plans... Before I could answer Cynthia confirms my return to New York once cleared medically.

Beth how did you and he leave things?

I struggle with finding words to explain how things were left. All I can manage to say ...I moved back to New York and he stayed in the good ole south.

And he hasn't been back to New York to see you?

If he's been to New York it hasn't been to see me… Can we change the subject now?

Chapter 9
Impossibilities

Not sure of the time we finally went to sleep and if Kevin even went to sleep. I scan the clock on the VCR, 6:30 a.m. ugh Kevin is up and fully dressed.

Hey..... Up so early?

This is late for me, *Kevin says with a smile.* But yes I'm meeting Erickson at seven this morning to go over a few things.

Getting up... Can I fix you coffee or something to eat?

Thanks but I already made coffee and right in front of you a fresh cup of tea.

Thank you... *and I smile.*

Beth what are your plans for today?

Just stay in and prepare myself for work tomorrow. Why?

Can you stay with your sister?

Kevin I am fine!

Yes you are *he says with a smile* but I'm concerned. Would you consider spending the day at my place?

Kevin I will be fine. I won't open the door for anyone.

You are one stubborn woman. I get off about six, can I come back here?

Kevin you clearly need some rest and you're not getting it here. GO HOME!

I would prefer stopping by to see you first if that is okay?

That would fine. I'll see you later today.

Kevin takes another sip of his coffee, picks up his gym bag and walks out the door. Ah Beth please come here now and lock the door… now… Please!

Are you kidding me Okay *When I reach the door Kevin gives a wink and says again* See you later today.

It is now 6:35 a.m. on a Sunday morning. I feel something furry at my feet Hey little guy, I guess I need to come up with a name huh. Hmm naming you Gizmo number two would be a bit unfair. How about Tiger? You like tiger? *In response I get a low pitch meow.* Tiger it is. Well let's get you something to eat. *I go into the kitchen to feed Tiger but I see Kevin beat me to it.* Not only has he fed you little man but he also washed and dried the mugs left in the sink. Huh... I bet not too many of his kind around. *I leave the kitchen and walk into my bedroom.*

Stretched across my bed I begin to plan my day. Maybe I should get out for a bit, do some grocery shopping, maybe pick up a few toys for you little guy? Swing by Cynthia's? I know she's pissed, I smile at the idea of seeing Cynthia upset with me. As much as she wants to be, her anger usually last until she physically sees me.

With my day planned, I hop into the shower. How good the hot water feels. As I'm lathering myself I begin to think about Detective Kevin Walker. What a fine looking man. Is he interested in me? Maybe, but Beth we don't do relationships and for him to become a fuck buddy, not in the cards. As quickly as I give thought is as quickly my inner self shut's it down.

With nothing more to fantasize about I begin to linger on what is happening around me. I wish I had some sort of clue behind it all. But I can't believe it is anyone I know personally, not even Michael. Maybe I should have been a bit more forthcoming regarding Hector. We definitely had our share of run-ins over the past few years. From birthday parties to Christmas but I think the worst was Easter 1997.....

March 30, 1997 - Easter Sunday

I arrive to Jasmine's house at 2 p.m. In hand an Easter basket for Rosie, flowers for Jasmine and Rosa, and a bunny sheet cake for all.

Tap… Tap…

Jasmine opens the door. Hey Beth glad you could make it.

Hi Jasmine thanks for having me. These are for you *handing Jasmine a bouquet of yellow roses.*

Thank you Beth, they are beautiful. Please come in.

I follow Jasmine to the back of her home, out the back door and into her backyard. Rosie greets me in a beautiful yellow ruffled dress. Her hair beautifully combed with Shirley Temple curls. Hello my little love *picking Rosie up and kissing her* how's my princess?

This for you Beth, *in hand Rosie gives me a small jewelry box. Enclosed is a locket.*

Rosie this is beautiful. Please tell me you put a picture of yourself inside?

Mommy did.

I open the locket and inside a picture of Rosie and Rosa. I love it. Now can you give this to your mom?

Pretty flowers

Yes and you tell her they are from you. Okay!

Rosie runs over to Rosa and hands Rosa the bouquet of Red long stemmed roses with two white roses in the center. Beth said from me but I didn't pay. *Everyone in hearing distance begin to laugh. I walk over and hug and kiss Rosa.*

Beth they are beautiful but you shouldn't have.

Rosie can you pull the white roses out for mommy?

Struggling, Rosie pulls the two white roses from the bouquet to reveal a necklace with a mommy charm.

With tears in her eyes Thank you Beth I love it but you really shouldn't have!

Well I did and where should I put the cake?

((Jasmine)) ((Jasmine))… where do you want Beth to put the cake?

Jasmine walks from inside the house and opens the box. Beth this is lovely. I'll bring it into the kitchen for later.

As Jasmine takes the cake in, I call Rosie back over. Okay Little Miss. Rosie, Happy Easter *and I hand Rosie her Easter Basket.*

Barbie…

Yes filled with all Barbie stuff. But before you take everything out, I need you to take out that small box.

This one?

Yup, can you open it?

In a flash Rosie un-wraps the box and opens it… Hello Kitty.

Yes Hello Kitty.

Put on?

We would need to ask mommy.

Walking toward Rosa, Rosie shows Rosa the earrings Beth you really shouldn't have.

Oh Rosa it is only Hello Kitty.

Can I put on?

Rosa with tears in her eyes takes the earrings Rosie has in her ears out and put the Hello Kitty earrings in Beautiful.

As the day continued, Jasmine, Rosie, Rosa and I talk about the events in the news, changes within city government and of course Rosie and how she is becoming such a little lady. However all conversation ended when Jasmine answered her door. It is Hector. From inside the house, I hear Jasmine screaming "Get out now" *Alarmed I jump up and hand Rosie to Rosa.*

Beth oh my God, what is he doing here?

I don't know. You stay back here with Rosie.

I walk into the house and Hector is arguing with Jasmine. Hey Hector what's going on?

Get the fuck out of here, you're here? And you *looking at Jasmine* have a problem with me being here?

Hector, do you recall the restraining order? You're not to be here.

Who made you the fucking judge?

Hector please just leave.

Leave?

Yes

But my mother came here to see her granddaughter?

Where is she?

What?

Where is she, your mother? I'm sure Jasmine would be okay if your mother came inside for a second to see her granddaughter. *Looking Jasmine in the face*

Why can't Rosie come out with me?

Hector because she can't.

This is bullshit… That is my mother fucking daughter.

Yes she is and no one is saying otherwise. *Hector's anger presents to be increasing, becoming more agitated. I open my cell phone in my pocket and press the number one which is preprogrammed for 911. I continue communicating with Hector, but now describing the scene for the 911 operator on the other the end of the line. Hector now yelling at both Jasmine and me, I yell back* Hector you're the one who came all the way to 2854 Myrtle Avenue, Jasmine's home without an invitation and with full knowledge of the rules outlined in the order of protection. *Jasmine with a puzzled look, Hector too involved in his rant does not realize what just occurred and within minutes three squad cars are outside the door.*

What the fuck. That bitch Rosa called the police.

No Hector I did.

You fucking bitch a*nd as Hector lunges for me, an officer grabs him and throws him to the floor.*

You fucking bitch, your day is coming. Hear me it is coming.

As one of the officers begins to take statements I walk outside expecting to be confronted by Hector's mother. But to my surprise no Mrs. Rodriguez. I look at Jasmine and then at Hector.

You sick fuck, your intent was to take her wasn't it? You stupid son of a bitch *and in a quick second I find myself slapping Hector straight across the face.*

You fucking bitch, I will have your job. Fucking Punta *ending his rage by spitting in my direction. Not that I am a fan of police brutality I was grateful for Hector's head meeting the top of the patrol car as the officer was putting him in. Done purposely I assume by the wink from the officer.*

Returning inside, both Rosie and Rosa are understandably upset. Dismissing what had occurred, I bring the Bunny cake out from the kitchen and pull sparkle candles from my purse. Seeing the candles Rosie shouts

Birthday… Birthday…

I turn to Rosie no today isn't anyone's birthday but because it is a special occasion special candles can be used. *I place the candles into the cake and light each one... From each candle a hissing sound affect occurs while each candle spins and glitters. A great ending to a hell of a day!*

Chapter 10
Truth of it All

Tap… Tap…

Who is it?

Mrs. Frankel it is Beth

After a few seconds Mrs. Frankel opens the door.

Hope I didn't wake you Mrs. Frankel but I wanted to see if you needed anything from the grocery store?

Beth you're not going out, are you?

Puzzled by Mrs. Frankel's response Yes I have a few errands to run.

But, that nice Detective, Kevin said you were going to be in all day?

Kevin? When did you speak to Kevin?

He came by this morning. Such a nice young man, he said he wanted to make sure I was ok. That is when he told me you would be home today.

Really! *This man…I should be pissed but…*

Yes Beth such a nice young man. You shouldn't disappoint him by going out.

Oh Mrs. Frankel, *remember she is an older woman, bite your tongue.* I won't be long. But to my original question, can I get you anything?

No Beth, I went shopping yesterday but thank you.

Alrighty, I'll be back soon.

Beth please come back by when you get home.

I will Mrs. Frankel. See you later.

I exit the building and head for my car. Once in I decide to hit Waldbaums first on Linden Place. Arriving at the supermarket an idea hits. Not that I can cook, I can at least offer Kevin a small meal to thank him for all that he has done these past few days. As much as I don't want to admit it, the company of another, the company of Kevin has been very helpful. So Baked chicken, garlic mashed potatoes, string beans and for dessert, lemon meringue pie. Sounds like a plan.

After about an hour, my grocery shopping is complete. I now head to the pet store just down the block. I purchase a few toys and a collar. Glancing over at litter pans I decide to purchase a cover for the pan Kevin provided for Tiger. Once again how astute on his part to remember that for some unbeknown reason, Gizmo's pan was taken along with all his other items. Okay I think I have all that I need and make my purchases. I pack all my items into my car and head over to Cynthia's.

Thank goodness the Whitestone expressway is empty for this time of day, on a Sunday. I Hope Sunrise Highway is the same. Arriving now to Cynthia's after about a 40 minute drive I already smell Sunday dinner being cooked. Where's my key? After about a minute of searching I find my key and enter. Stepping into the house I am greeted by my loving sister who was coming down the stairs.

What are you doing here Beth? *My sister's tone presenting as why have you brought your yellow ass to my house. I knew she would be upset with me initially but I know my sister. In a few minutes I will be her darling girl once again.*

Wow the love. I can't visit the woman who raised me? *I bear hug and kiss Cynthia.*

Really, all that? You don't know how to call people back huh!

Sorry Cynthia, been a little busy.

Hmmm, well get to talking *as she leads us to the kitchen.*

What would you like to talk about?

Don't play games Beth, what is going on?

I'm not, not much going on.

As she sets a teacup with a teabag in front of me, Cynthia glances that "don't mess with me bitch" look. Alright, alright Rosa and Rosie were killed a few days ago.

(((What))), that was the family?

Tears develop in Cynthia's eyes not for any relationship she had with Rosie and Rosa but for the close relationship I had. Are you okay?

I am… really.

Beth who did you talk to?

Shit I knew it was going to come to this, Cynthia I'm fine.

I didn't ask you that. Who did you call? Who did you see?

Not liking where this conversation is going I attempt to change the subject. So where's Ty?

With frustration on her face sleep, he worked late last night. Now do I need to repeat myself?

Cynthia I don't need to talk to anyone, I'm okay… getting thru it. *I end my conversation here. By the frustrated worried look increasingly growing on Cynthia's face I dare not review Gizmo's death or the break in. No it would be best to leave matters as is.*

Beth holding the world on your shoulders DOESN'T WORK... *And as Cynthia begins her I don't know what, my cell rings from a number I do not recognize.*

Hello?

Beth what the hell are you doing?

Huh? Kevin?

Yes I thought you were staying in?

What the fuck, I realized I needed to do some shopping. Wait, how do you know I'm out?

Mrs. Frankel called. She was concerned that you weren't back from the store by now.

How did she get your number? *As the words were coming out of my mouth I answered my own foolish question. Of course he gave her his number.*

Beth, where are you?

I'm at my sister's house.

What is the address?

What? Why do you need that?

Beth what is the address?

Glancing over at Cynthia my eyes zoom in on the "Lucy you got some splainin to do" look. Ha yes I get a kick out of myself. Kevin I'm about to leave now. *In a whisper* I'm heading home and all will be fine. *Not giving him a chance to respond I hang up.*

Beth a lot more is going on than what you are telling me. I do not like this, not one bit. Who just called you?

Huh?

Do not play dumb. Dumb you are not!

Taking a sip of my now prepared cup of tea then what am I?

Beth no time for games!

As Cynthia continues to question me, I walk over to the stove and begin tasting what she has prepared for Sunday dinner. On the counter the world's best potato salad can I take some with me?

Without skipping a Beat, her now anger questioning continues as she prepares a bowl for me to take. But in the middle of preparing me a goody bag I officially get the authoritative, matriarch of the family. Cynthia has the look of pure frustration on her face. Usually along with this look one should brace themselves because in this moment she will clearly express how she feels. No mixing of words, no sugar coating.

Beth, stop the bullshit. What the fuck is going on?

Cynthia, don't worry about me. I'm good.

Beth!!!!

Cynthia I have to live life and I need you to trust my coping skills. *Little does she know my skills include Mr. Absolute!*

With tears streaming down her face, Cynthia grabs me by both my arms and shakes me. Beth promise me on daddy, promise me you will talk to someone.

She pulled the daddy card. Really low I will Cynthia but I am ok.

Beth, who do you think you are fooling? *Tears begin to trickle down her face.* I know how you felt about Rosa and her daughter. I know what they meant to you so stop all the bullshit and talk to me.

Cynthia I'm okay. Yes it hit me pretty hard initially but I'm okay. No need to worry about me.

Someone has to!

While Cynthia continues to vent her feelings on this matter I begin to pack up what she has prepared for me to take home.

Can you at least stay for dinner?

No Cynthia I have a few errands to run but I greatly appreciate what you packed for me. *Cynthia's goody bag consists of very large portions of whatever she has prepared for dinner. Completely packed up now, I pick up my goody bag, kiss and hug my sister and head for the door.* You know I love you more than anyone knows.

No Beth, you need to know I love you with everything. You're my baby girl. I would not be able to handle if.....

Knowing what the "if" is referring to, I whisper I'm here and nowhere near that place. *I wipe her tears away and slap her ass. I then inquire if anyone else is slapping that ass and we both begin to laugh. Walking out the door Cynthia yells, (((*I love you Beth))). *I yell back,* (((You're the wind beneath my wings))). *We both laugh and I'm on my way home.*

I pull up to my building about 1:15 p.m. My stomach begins to flip. A patrol car is sitting in front of the building. Getting out of my car my cell rings again from that unfamiliar number.

Hello?

Beth, nice to hear your home

Let me guess, you have the patrol car here? What a waste of my tax paying dollars.

Beth not now! The car will remain in place.

Why, did something happen?

No, but one of the two people on this call seems to have difficulty keeping to a planned agenda.

Not amused, I guess my safety has been confirmed and you can go directly home and get some rest!

No Beth, I stick to a plan. I will see you when I get off *and the line goes dead.*

What the fuck, better yet who the fuck. Making two trips in, I grab items from my car, each time being the smartass that I am, waving to the officers.

Already 5:15 p.m. Cooking complete and table set. Kevin should be arriving soon and just as I complete my thought, someone is ringing my buzzer.

Who is it?

Beth its Kevin

Okay… *and I buzz him in.*

Tap… Tap…

I swing open the door.

Detective Walker

Mrs. Morris

So is this how your visit is going to go? *Asking with bit of an attitude.*

No Beth, not at all. I hope you realize what you did or better yet what you haven't.

Trying to hold back a smile, one begins to surface.

I'm glad I can provide you with entertainment.

Oh come on, can you really be upset? If anything I should be the one with a pissy attitude.

You think so?

Think so no, know so absolutely. But look I don't want to argue.

Neither do I Beth!

Then great because I prepared a small dinner to thank you for all you have done over the past few days.

You cooked?

Don't sound so surprise *I say with a smile.* I hope you like baked chicken, homemade mac and cheese, potato salad and to cap it off, lemon meringue pie?

Yes, yes and heck yes.

Great *walking into the kitchen Kevin follows*

Wow Beth!

Yes wow… Now if you wouldn't mind taking a seat at the table I will bring dinner in.

Sitting at the table Beth this looks amazing and smells delicious.

I hope after tasting you feel the same.

I'm sure I will.

As Kevin and I eat, I inquire about Kevin's background. Originally from Alabama moved to New York when he was sixteen. Ha that clarifies the ever so politeness. Graduated from Colgate University then Columbia, achieving a Master's in Forensic Psychology. Joined the New York City Police Department twelve years ago. When inquiring about his parents - siblings, Kevin explained he is an only child and was raised by his grandparents. At this point Kevin stops talking about himself and reflects the attention to me. The questioning begins.

Beth what happen with you and your ex-husband?

Excuse me? Where is this coming from?

What happen?

Nothing happened. The relationship just didn't work.

As the last words are coming out my mouth, I notice a painful – sorrow look on Kevin's face.

Kevin what is wrong?

Grabbing my arms and turning to look at my wrists, a rush of embarrassment overcomes me. I yank my arms away, stand and head into the kitchen. How could he know? Cynthia? She would never ever share this part of my life with anyone. When it happened Cynthia and my dad were very discreet. For the short time I stayed with Cynthia, no visitors. I don't even think she told Ty or Jay. What the fuck. As I pour a glass of vodka, Kevin comes into the kitchen and grabs my hand.

Stop, this isn't going to take anything away.

With Tears streaming down my face and anger in my voice, how did you find out about this?

Pulling my head up to look at him and wiping away my tears, I ran a check on Michael.

I shake my head no and remove myself from his gaze.

Beth I had to. Can you tell me what happen?

I'm sure your report tells it all.

I would rather hear from you.

That won't happen today *before Kevin could reply his cell phone rings.*

Walker

Not understanding the whole conversation but it seems he needs to get back to Brooklyn. I'll see you in twenty. *Kevin walks back toward me and in hand a file folder.* Enclosed is the information sent from Greensboro. *He hands me the file.* I have to meet my partner but I would like to stay here tonight?

Look you have a car out front.

Yes I do and it will remain in place. So can I?

With tears trickling, I don't appreciate pity.

And I don't give it. So I will call you on my way back. *Not waiting for a response, Kevin is out the door, closing the door behind himself.*

With folder in hand, I debate with myself, should I read it? Since the day of I've never read the police report never even testified in court nor witnessed sentencing. There was no need. To my understanding he turned himself in and pled guilty. I toss the file onto the table and begin washing the dinner dishes. Trying to keep my mind off the file I sit on the couch and prepare myself for tomorrow's workday.

Wow seven-thirty already? I'll prepare the couch for Kevin. Gathering fresh linen and adding a pillow from my bed I lay the items across the couch. In the bathroom I leave a towel, wash cloth, toothpaste, and a toothbrush. I enter my bedroom and prepare myself for a shower and bed. I pull out a night shirt and slipper socks. I have to laugh, even if I had a reason to put on something sexy, wouldn't be found here. I head to the bathroom passing the dining table. No longer able to ignore the obvious I pick up the file and enter the bathroom. Instead of showering I decide to take a hot bath which allows me time to sit and review a time in my life I hope one day to forget. I begin running the water and stripping off my clothes. I step into the hot bath with file in hand. I begin my read.

Initial Police Report

Case Number: **GBPD -10-64010**

Incident**: Domestic Disturbance / Possible Suicide Attempt**

Reporting Officer: **Deputy Patrick D. O'Brien**

Date of Report: **11/24/1988 at 11:29 p.m.**

On November 24, 1988 at 11:29 p.m. I, Deputy Patrick D. O'Brien was dispatched to 17 Kramer Road Greensboro, North Carolina in conjunction with Emergency Medical Services. First on the scene, this writer rang doorbell as well as knocked on the front door. No answer. This writer then proceeded to walk to the back of the house where a male voice screaming for help was heard. This writer then proceeded to enter home by way of unlocked patio door.

Upon entering I announced who I am and in response a male voice (Michael Morris) informed me where he was. Entering the bathroom I found an African American Male (Michael Morris) kneeling over a nude fair skin African American female who presented not to be conscious. Female also presented to be bleeding from wrists and thigh areas. Significant bruises – hand print around neck, hand print on both left and right face cheeks and bloody nose.

Within minutes of my arrival EMS arrived and began CPR as well as attending to proclaimed self-inflicted (as reported by husband, Michael Morris) cut wounds. During the time the Emergency Medical Technicians were treating female I began questioning Mr. Morris regarding current situation. Mr. Morris sated he arrived home around 11:20 p.m. and found his wife laying on the bathroom floor nude, covered in blood and non - responsive. When inquiring if he knew what happen here tonight, Mr. Morris stated no. When attempting to question further Mr. Morris declined to provide any further information due to his stated need to be with his wife.

It should be noted that the home was without electricity and heat. Walking through the home broken glass was found in the living area. This writer has already alerted house detective for further investigating. Case remains active.

That lying son of a bitch! He came home and found me that way? He lied! All the more reason to hate this man!

Detective Follow-up Report

Case Number: **GBPD -10-64010 -02**

Incident**: Domestic Disturbance / Possible Suicide Attempt**

Reporting Officer: **Detective Carter Harris**

Date of Report: **11/26/1988 at 1:30 p.m.**

At 1:30 p.m. I Detective Carter P. Harris met with Elizabeth Morris at Saint Anne's Hospital. During this time Elizabeth Morris reviewed incident that occurred on November 24, 1988 which resulted in Emergency Services being called by Michael Morris, husband. Mrs. Morris informed this writer of the events that occurred on November 24, 1988.

Michael Morris arrived home approximately at nine o'clock in the evening. Reportedly (via Elizabeth Morris) intoxicated, Michael Morris began hitting / slapping Elizabeth Morris at least four times in the face and grasping Elizabeth Morris by the neck, holding her in place for several minutes. When she - Elizabeth Morris, attempted to leave the home Elizabeth Morris reports being dragged back into the house. Elizabeth Morris also reviewed being forced to engage in sexual intercourse. However, cuts to wrist and thigh confirmed by Mrs. Morris as self-inflicted, stating "To end what I am going through - taking my life seemed like the only way I would get peace".

Based on information provided, a warrant for the arrest of Michael Morris requested. Charges: Domestic Abuse, Rape and false imprisonment.

Written Wavier

Court Plea

Defendant: I Michael Robert Morris enter a plea of guilty to the charge of second degree assault against Elizabeth Morris on December 12, 1988. I waive my right to a jury trial and accept sentencing as reviewed with me by my attorney. I understand and agree to five years' probation, mandated weekly individual and group counseling and will sustain from any contact with Elizabeth Morris.

Well just basic information in both. I'm sort of relieved to the generalization and not so detailed. But realistically I was the one who had the details and I guess my lack of cooperation during this time did not help. If I knew then Michael's lie I probably would have stayed and fought this out. But all I wanted then was to get out of North Carolina and start over, which I did? And the pregnancy, as explained by Detective Harris, if mentioned on record, the possibility of charging me for ... well charging me for what I did – killing another. Between Cynthia, Detective Harris and the attorney

Cynthia hired, the pregnancy information only noted in medical file.

Upon ending my bath, my buzzer rings. Making my way to the living room I inquire who it is.

Who is it?

Hi Beth, Kevin.

I buzz Kevin in. I unlock my door and go into my bedroom to dress. Several seconds later I hear Kevin in the living room.

Why is the door is unlocked and open Beth?

Yelling from my bedroom, (((To let you in)))

Beth you cannot do that....

………....

Do you hear me?

Walking out of my bedroom, to the living room I yell ((YES)). *When I enter the living room Kevin is standing by the door...* What's wrong?

Nothing Beth

Then why are you waiting by the door?

Just waiting to be invited in.

Really? *With a smile...*I guess you will need an invite to sleep with me I mean sleep here tonight?

Embarrassment must be written all over my face.

With a smile, I think I already have permission.

Ignoring his reply Can I get you something to eat or cup of coffee?

Beth a cup of coffee would be great.

Heading into the kitchen I notice Kevin to be deep in thought, as if he had troubling news. Kevin, can I fix you a sandwich to go along with your coffee?

No… No thank you Beth only coffee.

Bringing Kevin his coffee I sit beside him on the couch. Kevin's expression and demeanor presents very different from the man I've been getting to know?

Thank you Beth and Beth *stuttering a bit*, I apologize for this afternoon. I had no right to keep questioning you.

Kevin, that part of my life, what I did.... *trying not to cry but tears begin falling* I am very ashamed of.

Putting his arm around me and caressing my back, Beth I am so sorry.

Sorry *repeated with a giggle,* you have nothing to be sorry for.

I spoke with the detective on the case *Kevin's voice cracking* He told me you were severely beaten and pregnant?

That ole feeling of shame hovers above me like a rain cloud, yes and as you are already aware, I attempted to take my life. *Hearing my own words I begin to shake uncontrollably. Attempting to get up from where I'm sitting Kevin pulls me back down beside him, holding me firm.*

Beth, are you okay?

……………

Beth?

Kevin I just need a few minutes to myself.

Beth talk to me *Kevin's facial expression is one I've seen a few times over, the uncertainty of doing harm to oneself if left alone.*

I smile at Kevin and stand Kevin no worries, needing time to myself doesn't translate into "I can't handle life and I'm going to off myself".

Not knowing if he should call 911 or follow me, Kevin stands and we are now eye to eye. Beth, this evening when you asked about my upbringing I told you my grandparents raised me. The reason, my mother took her life when I was four years old. *Tears forming in his eyes.* Just know I miss her every day of my life. I'm not a Psychiatrist but know when ending your life for whatever the reason, will affect, no ruin the life of everyone close to you, who loves you. You may assume that people close to you will understand why you did what you did but in reality, they don't.

Tears streaming down my face I grab Kevin by his hand and then put my arms around him, hugging him very tight. No other words am I able to form or verbalize, just his name. I begin to weep and Kevin begins hugging me completely. He whispers in my ear "you're not alone regardless how difficult life seems".

Taking a deep breath I begin collecting myself. I hug Kevin once more and whisper thank you.

Looking him straight in his eyes, Kevin takes my face in his hand, rubs my right cheek and kisses me. His lips touching mine I begin to resist internally, a battle brewing from within. Oh how badly I wanted this from this man who is here with me now. But I don't want a relationship, I can't do a relationship. I haven't had one since Michael. I am afraid to… just afraid. Taking direction from my inner voice, I pull away.

Why are you pulling away?

Kevin I don't do relationships

Beth?

Kevin I don't.

Beth do you know I've been attracted to you from the first time I laid my eyes on you and every day since I look forward to seeing you?

Kevin stop!

Beth, I'm not asking for anything. But know I am here if you need anything.

Kevin, thank you but I can't…

Beth, just know I'm here *and along with his last words Kevin again kisses me but this time on my forehead. He releases me from his hold.*

Trying to suppress my internal battle I walk into my bedroom and close the door. In the dark I sit on my bed and digest what just occurred. Trying to convince myself to take a chance with Kevin, to for once in eleven years take stock in what a man is telling me and not dissect each and every word to make it an untruth, a un-possibility. How my heart needed this right now especially since the two people who seemed to fill this void is gone, no longer here with me. Beth he seems like a good man. You thought Michael was a good man. For each good quality I identify in Kevin I instantly pick it away, comparing to Michael. Oh God how I wish I could give myself to someone without fear that I not only will be hurt physically by another but me hurting myself from not being able to deal. Not liking where my thoughts are taking me, I fall to my knees and plead with God to give me strength, make me strong and allow me right this moment to walk and no longer crawl. My pleading comes to a halt due to a knock on my door.

Beth?

Kevin I'll be out in a few

Beth can I come in? *Seeming not to wait for a response Kevin opens the door and walks to where I am.* I guess we have something in common.

Excuse me? *Confused by his statement*

We both ask for guidance when our hearts are heavy, weighing us down.

Smiling with tears flowing, I guess we do. *As I stand to my feet Kevin extends his hand to help me up.*

Beth let's watch a little TV?

Sounds good to me.

We walk out to the living room and re-establish the seating from the night before. We begin watching the 11:00 p.m. news. But shortly into the broadcast I find myself feeling safe and serene once again, I drift into a comfortable slumber.

Chapter 11
Back to Business

Sitting here at my desk I have so much to do but no focus to give. I knew it would be hard coming here today but I never imagined it would be this difficult. All around me thirty-eight drawings, counted over and over again thirty-eight drawings from my Little Rosie. On the left of my desk, a photo of Rosie with Santa, on the right a photo of Rosie with the Easter Bunny and mid center, straight damn center a picture of Rosa, Rosie and me at Fresh Meadows Halloween Haunted Hay Ride. A smile surfaces upon my face just from the thought of this day. Nothing spectacular occurred, just the remembrance of togetherness. While deep in thought I hear a tap on my door.

Tap... Tap...

Come in

Hi Beth, how are you?

Well I made it all the way to 10:00 a.m. before anyone asked the infamous question I'm fine Rochelle, what's been going on around here?

Fine really Beth?

Unsure if the look on Rochelle's face is pity or frustration. Yes...

Well then maybe you can explain why the District Attorney's office subpoenaed our records, more specifically records on cases you specifically worked on?

What?

It was also recommended that your field work be limited until…

Limited, until when?

Not sure Beth. Why didn't you tell me your home was broken into?

What was there to tell Rochelle?

Beth..... Come on....

Really, what should I have said?

Beth I thought you and I had a better relationship then this.

We do Rochelle, which is why I did not want you to worry over something that you did not need to worry over.

Really! I told Detective Walker your community visits would be on hold until he feels the matter is resolved.

Rochelle you can't do that, I have several appointments and

Abruptly interrupted "You had" Beth. No fieldwork and I mean it. Pam and I will cover whatever needs to be covered.

Before I could even attempt to argue the matter, Rochelle was out my office with door closed behind her. What am I going to do now? Sit in this damn office day after day? With my anger building internally I pick up the phone and call dear Detective Walker. He got me into this and he is going to insure these ridiculous restrictions are lifted.

Ring… Ring...

Walker…

Kevin?

Beth is everything okay? *Sounding anxious*

No Kevin it certainly is not. I need you to call Rochelle and let her know all is fine.

But everything isn't fine Beth

Kevin, I can't do my job by sitting in the office all day. I have families to see, home visits.

Beth I understand how you feel but until we find out who is behind what is going on, no field work.

This is absolutely ridiculous.

Ridiculous or not, no field work.

Whatever… I have to go.

Beth?

…………

Beth!

((Yes)) *Sounding annoyed*

Making sure we are still on for this evening?

Hmmm

Beth?

Yes I guess

Well, I'll take that response and run with it. See you at six.

The thought of seeing him again this evening put a smile on my face. See you then…

And Beth, remember if you need anything, I'm just a phone call away.

Hmmm you're lucky I'm talking to you now… *I chuckle...* See you this evening.

Kevin chuckles as well but I imagine a very handsome smile on his face. Yes I am lucky and I hope my luck continues for a very long time. See you later.

With an even bigger smile upon my face see you later.

Seems talking to Kevin perked up my mood a bit and the idea of meeting him for dinner and a movie this evening gave me something to look forward to. I begin looking through mail that piled up over the past few days I was out. Looking through I notice the mail had already been open? Looked through? Puzzled I get up from my desk and walk out to the reception area where Paige's desk is located.

Hey Paige

Hi Beth, everything okay? Need something?

Not sure, I was looking through my mail and notice it all had been open?

Oh yeah sorry Beth, I should have told you. The police have been by a few times looking at records, mail etc. Usually two Detectives. A Detective Walker and a Detective Erickson.

Really!

Yes, and all our calls both office and cells are being monitored. Rochelle didn't tell you any of this?

No she didn't *but neither did that son of a bitch Detective Walker. Trying to suppress my desperate need to yell* Paige anything more I missed or should know?

With a look of I'm afraid to share anything more Ah yes one more thing

Go ahead… *I say with suppressed sarcasm*

Your paycheck - would you like it?

Ah, yes I would *feeling a bit bad.* Paige I apologize for any tone in my voice.

Beth I understand.

I return to my office and begin working on Ms. Black's case, calling around for open housing opportunities then calling Roy Wilkins Community Center for possible day care and pre-school openings. By the end of the day, I see the product of my persistence. I call Ms. Black and review what was accomplished and what remains pending. By the end of my call, Ms. Black ask if I could stop by tomorrow to see her. Without hesitance I schedule to meet at nine in the morning. I will just notify Rochelle in the morning as I'm driving to the shelter. Better yet, I will call before the office opens and leave a message on her voice mail. Now that I have my well thought out plan, I pack my briefcase and begin to head out. Just as I'm about to leave

Beth you have a call on line one.

Picking up line one Beth Morris

Hi… Beth

Yes Detective Walker, how can I help you?

I'm Detective Walker now, hmmm.

Any reason you didn't tell me about your involvement with my office?

I had a feeling

Feeling? Feeling about what? *Expressed with pure anger* that I would find out from anyone but you about the mail and phones?

Beth, I'm not going to apologize for this. You and I have jobs that we both must do. My number one priority right now is to find a killer before anyone else is harmed.

But you could have said something

No Beth.

Crazy but now I'm even more so attracted to this man. So Detective Walker, what do you want from me right this minute.

I want you to know… I can't wait to see you and spend time with you this evening.

As much as I want to remain angry I can't. Kevin's last words put an ever so large smile on my face. I look forward to seeing you too. See you soon *and I hang up. Not giving him an opportunity to say anything more to make me blush or better yet feel bad for my anger.*

During my train ride to Seventy First and Continental I begin to second-guess myself. Why am I meeting up with Kevin? I'm not looking for a relationship and I refuse to allow whatever this thing is to become physical? I can't! But maybe I'm debating a mute issue. Maybe Kevin is just not into me, looking for a fuck buddy himself? And what a fuck buddy he would probably be. Becoming completely lost in thought regarding Kevin in general, I look at the woman sitting across from me who seems to be staring at me. Once our eyes meet she says

You must be deep in thought and thinking of something very good because your facial expression for the past ten minutes has been one large smile.

I laugh out loud and reply just thinking of someone. *Both embarrassed and amused I now try to keep a straight face.*

By the time I'm able to clear my mind of Kevin, I've not only made it to my stop, I'm also off the train and made my way to the movie theater where I see Detective Kevin Walker standing, looking ever so handsome.

Good evening Detective Walker

Good evening Mrs. Morris. I must say you look mighty beautiful this evening.

Trying not to blush... Thank you.

You're looking quite dapper yourself. *What I really want to say is damn you look so good.*

Well thank you *he says with a gorgeous smile*. I already purchased the tickets so let's head in.

Ah excuse me, this evening is on me. Do you recall me stating so last night?

I do recall Beth but to remind you, I agreed that whoever arrived first would pay.

Wow, really sneaky especially since I arrived a few minutes early to insure that I was first.

Ha, yes I was sure that was going to be your plan, but I was once told that the early bird gets the worm....

Really Mr. Walker!

Oh now I'm Mr. Walker. I sense a pattern here. If called Mr. Walker I know I'm in trouble.

Both Kevin and I begin to laugh. The gentleman he presents to be, Kevin loops his arm into mine and we begin walking entwined, side by side into the theater.

Sitting and watching Austin Powers, I find myself eyeing every move Kevin makes. So far his arm was around my chair, then he shifts and it is back on his lap. Did I give him reason to move it? Oh he is shifting again... Wait hmmm he's holding my hand now. Thank goodness for the darkness because I must be beat red. No longer concentrating at all on the movie, I begin wondering about the "what if's" If he is going to ask again to stay over? If he makes a move this evening, what will I do? If I will allow myself to take the next step? So many "what ifs" and no answers. By the time I end of my "what if's" battle, the movie is over.

So what did you think about the movie?

Oh boy, I hope I saw enough to answer questions... Very funny?

I thought so too. Okay how about some dinner?

Kevin I will agree to eat a meal with you if and only if *(another if... I laugh internally)* I PAY!

Mrs. Morris I'm not going to debate this issue, you pay for yours and I will pay for mine.

Still not happy *I say sternly* I would like to pay for you also?

Sure, no fight from me. There's a great Chinese restaurant about a block up, how does that sound to you?

Sounds like a plan.

As Kevin and I walk to the restaurant, Kevin talks about the movie and his favorite parts. Unable to really describe any parts due to my lack of focus during the movie, I just laugh and agree. Arriving to the restaurant about five minutes later, we are seated in a private booth.

You must come here often huh.

I've been here a few times but why do you assume I frequent this place?

Well by the way the hostess greeted you.

Kevin, seeming to hold back a smile I've been here a few times.

Interesting *I reply in a sarcastic tone. As I'm about to inquire a bit more, a waitress comes over with a bouquet of long stem roses and hands them to me.*

Ah I don't think these are for me.

Kevin with a straight face, See a card?

Turning the bouquet around I find a small card. "Beautiful roses for a beautiful woman. I hope we have many more times out together" Signed Kevin

Wow Mr. Walker…

Oh no I hear Mr. Walker so I guess I'm in a bit of trouble.

By far, you are not. The roses are lovely, thank you.

You're very welcomed but please note, I mean what I wrote, hope this is a beginning of us getting to know one another.

Gees this conversation just took a big turn into left field, getting a bit too serious for me right now. But here I go again, pulling away from possible happiness. I can't do this now. So what do you think about those Mets?

With a look of "Hello I just gave you a piece of me and you ask about the fucking Mets" coldly responds Not much of a Mets fan.

Oh… are you into sports at all?

Basketball

Did I piss him off? Your favorite team?

Bulls

Bulls really? You do know you live in New York!!

Very aware, but I haven't seen a rulebook that states you have to root for the home team.

Your right no rule book but as a true New Yorker, Knicks all the way … *In a whisper...* even if they suck most of the time.

While sipping his wine, Kevin almost spits his wine out in response to my whisper. We both begin to laugh.

After about an hour or so we are finally ready to go. Kevin excuses himself to use the restroom. I begin to panic internally with what - how should or should not offer him to come in for a drink? Stay for a few minutes or the boldest of all choices, offer him to stay over. Before I could further debate and crown the winner I see Kevin walking back toward the table. As he is walking toward the table the waitress too walks by.

Ah excuse me, can we have the check?

Check… No check, bill paid.

Excuse me?

Your friend paid already.

With a look of annoyance I stare Kevin down as he walks toward the table. So you paid the tab?

Who me? Nah... Come on let's go.

Just when you gained several brownie points for such a wonderful evening!

Oh come on… *he extends his hand to help me up.*

Walking to the parking garage I once again internally debate the issue of next steps and the what if's. Deep in thought, I guess I've been ignoring what Kevin has been saying during the drive home, realizing he had asked a question by the tap on my hand.

Wow I wish I knew what you are thinking about.

Huh? Why?

Because you really seem deep in thought!

Oh, if he only knew.

So, is it okay?

Is what ok?

Wow you really weren't listening.

So sorry, what was the question?

Do you mind staying at my apartment this evening?

Eek I guess I have no choice but to visit this matter. But before I could even process an answer my mouth opens. Kevin sorry I have an early start tomorrow and I have to prepare a bit.

Beth please, don't think I would become fresh with you?

Ha ha ha. How old are you? Fresh with me? No, I did not take it that way *although deep down I want you to get FRESH with me.*

Well then can I stay at your place?

Kevin, why the need? I'm fine… Nothing to worry about!

Beth, when will you realize this isn't a joke, real things are happening to your real life? *In an instant Kevin's demeanor becomes agitated, upset.*

Why are you getting upset?

Beth upset would not be the word I use to describe how I feel, more like frustrated. But if you're not going to take what is going on around you, to you seriously… someone has to.

Kevin, I'm fine let's change the subject!

Wow when the kitchen becomes a bit too warm

Don't, do not think of finishing that sentence *I try to say with a straight face but I'm unable to suppress my laughter.*

Your one thickheaded woman Mrs. Morris.

Why thank you Detective Kevin Walker.

No other words spoken until we arrive at my apartment building.

Can I at least walk you up?

You can even come in for a cup of coffee.

So are my remaining brownie points being cashed in right now?

You bet they are.

Sitting on my couch, Kevin and I sit in awkward silence. I attempt to break the silence by asking how his day was. Kevin who seemed not to have been paying attention continued to look thru me rather at me. My question goes unanswered and I tap Kevin on his shoulder.

Kevin, come back to earth.

Huh...

Kevin do you have something on your mind?

Just a long day but back to my earlier question, can I stay over?

I thought we settled this already?

No wasn't resolved

Kevin I do not see the sense of it but if you would like the couch for another night it is yours.

Thank you!

Laughing let me get you what you need. *I walk into my bedroom and pull my spare comforter from my trunk. Once again the internal debate resumes. Should I pursue this any further? If I could receive some sort of sign from above. Heading back to the living area, I see Kevin nodding a bit. Deprived sleep definitely due to his protective need over me. Trying not to wake him, I put the comforter over him. Walking away I feel Kevin taking my hand into his.*

I didn't mean to wake you.

You didn't.

Well you get some sleep. I will see you in the morning.

Beth I have a small request, do you mind sitting with me to listen to a little music or watch TV?

Sure, let me change. *I go into my bedroom and change into an oversize tee shirt and a pair of slipper socks. I slip on my robe and head back out to the living area.*

10:00 O'clock news is on, do you mind if I turn it on…

No Beth, please watch.

I sit beside Kevin and we both submerge under the comforter. Kevin if it is too cool for you I can turn down the air conditioner.

No I'm fine.

Sitting here, both Kevin and I fall asleep. I'm awakened by the Honeymooners theme song. Trying not to wake Kevin I begin to untangle myself from his hold. Twisting from under his arm I find myself face to face with Kevin. Oh how handsome this man is and his scent. Moving in a bit closer to smell his neck I feel Kevin's arms come around me and his mouth locks onto mine. Oh God what am I doing and more importantly what was I going to allow myself to do. Forcing myself to pull away from Kevin, I pull up and stand in front of him.

Beth I did not mean any disrespect

I know… *Walking now away from him toward my bedroom I turn back to face Kevin.* Are you coming?

With a hesitant look on his face Are you sure?

I'm very sure *and I extend my hand for his. Hand in hand we walk into my bedroom. In this moment my doubts are no longer a concern. In this moment, I've never been surer of what I wanted... In this moment I want this man. I want to give myself physically to him. My wish, wants and needs are all about to become fulfilled. I give myself completely to this man, Kevin Walker.*

Chapter 12
Dissolving Bliss

Feeling the heat of the sun upon my face I wake in Kevin's masculine but very soft arms. Oh how long it has been since feeling utterly safe, serene and completely relaxed. Trying to move as little as possible I turn my head slightly upwards to take in Kevin's beautiful face, but only to my surprise I find Kevin looking down at me. His lips sporting that same devilish smile that appeared upon his face several times last night and early this morning. His eyes still glistening with both compassion and satisfaction.

Good Morning Detective Walker *I say with deep gratitude and satisfaction.*

Good Morning Mrs. Morris. How did you sleep?

Very well thank you *sporting a very large smile*

I concur *Kevin replies as he leans down and kisses me passionately.*

Detective Walker please do not start something I cannot finish.

With a big grin on his face we could finish…

What time is it? *Realizing it had to be after seven.*

Seven fifteen a.m.

Jumping up Oh crap I have to get up… Aren't you late for work?

Pulling me back down to him, yes for the first time in 12 years I'm late for work.

With a smile larger than life upon my face Oh Kevin I am so sorry.

Beth no worries, no worries at all! I had an extraordinary evening. The movie, dinner and last night, I couldn't ask for anything more.

Well I'm glad you enjoyed but I have to get up and dress before I'm late. Un-like you I've been late plenty of times.

With both of us laughing, I get up, go into the bathroom and turn on the shower. Kevin standing in my bedroom doorway

Kevin, would you want to go in first?

Would I be pushing my luck if I request we go in together?

This is your lucky day but no hanky panky. I have to get to work.

My lady just being next to you gives me satisfaction.

Kevin words put a smile upon my face but seeing this man completely nude, showing his perfected caramel skin tone with bulging triceps and ever so tight stomach makes me want more of him.
The shower water hits him as if hitting an orchid during a rain shower. Each drop slowly trickles down, finding its way from the top of his head down to his feet. Oh this man is so beautiful. I can't resists from starting what I previously stated would not be. No I needed this for me and I needed it now. Kevin in front I begin rubbing his back. I motion for him to face me. I see why he felt the need to be in front, this way I did not see his excitement and excited he is.

Mr. Walker would that happen to be for me?

I would love to offer it but I made a promise, no hanky panky!

Well I need to recant that statement Mr. Walker because I not only need you right this second but also want you right now.

Well my lady I am here to please…

By 8:15 both Kevin and I are showered and dressed.

Beth you're in the office today correct?

Huh? *Acting as if I'm not paying attention.*

Beth? You're in the office today correct?

You are correct Detective Walker. *A little white lie but it is better than the latter.*

Walking to our cars parked in front of the building, Kevin grabs me by the waist, pulls me into him and plants another passionate kiss upon my lips.

Kevin I can't take too many more of those kisses.

You? You just don't know what you do to me Elizabeth Morris.

The feeling is mutual Detective Walker.

We kiss once again, I climb into my car and Kevin closes the door. Squatting down near the driver side, Kevin motions for me to roll down my window.

Can I make a request?

I guess *curious as to what he will request*

Could you meet me at my apartment this evening?

By now you must be tired of me.

You don't understand Beth, I don't get enough of you!

With a smile on my face, yes I will stop by, around six?

Yes, and incase I'm not home let yourself in. Here are my keys.

Kevin attempts to hand me his keys but instantly I push them back into his hand.

Kevin I can wait until you get home.

But I don't want you to. Just let yourself in.

Kevin, No I can't!

Damn it. Will you ever just accept something or comply with a request without an argument? Yes you can and you will *tossing his house keys into the passenger seat of my car.* Have a wonderful day because I know I will.

You make me blush like a teenager *really no reason to inform him of this because my red face tells it all.*

Good… See you later.

As I'm pulling off Kevin blows me a kiss.

Getting onto the Whitestone expressway, I call the office and leave a message for Rochelle, confirming I'm meeting with Ms. Black this morning and would be in the office after. I know I will have to deal with the repercussions of my again blatant defiance, but I'm sure Rochelle will understand my defiance is in response to doing my job. Plus who is Kevin to say where and when I can go somewhere. I smile when I say his name. God I just pray this last longer than a second and for the time we are together, if I can call it that, we enjoy being with one another. It's been a very long time since I felt this way for someone and certainly a long time since I have given myself to anyone physically.

I arrive to the Shelter, pulling up to the front of the building I see Ms. Black standing outside with the kids.

Good Morning Angela, is everything ok?

Oh, yes Beth I was waiting for someone.

Oh… okay. So where do you want to meet?

Beth the reason why I asked you to come by wasn't for me but a woman I met a few weeks ago.

And how do you think I could assist this woman?

The last time you came to see me I went to the park with the kids after. Within a few minutes of us being in the park a woman walked up to me and asked if you were helping me.

Helping you?

That was my same response. She then told me she had nowhere to live and her boyfriend physically abuses her and her one year old daughter.

And she was to meet you here? Now?

Yes I saw her, Karen yesterday and she said she would meet me here. We were to meet at 8:30.

Any idea where she lives?

No, but Beth I've seen her a few times coming out of the abandon house across the street.

Let's wait here for a few minutes to see if she comes.

While waiting the twins begin crying. Attempting to assist Ms. Black I pick up one of the twins with hopes of comforting her but my efforts are in vein. Both Angela and I each have one of the little girls. Unfortunately holding each in no way soothes or comforts them. Instead the crying actually becomes louder.

Beth I am really sorry. They *(referring to her twin daughters)* are teething.

Maybe you should get them inside.

Beth I'm sorry for asking you to come all this way. If I see her again I will give her your number.

That's fine. Come on I will help you inside

Beth I am truly sorry.

Don't be. You're trying to help someone.

Thanks Beth.

After walking Ms. Black into the building, I decide to wait a few more minutes, sitting in my car across from the abandon house. The thought of someone living in such conditions and with a young child, a baby suppress my eagerness to get to the office. Within about five minutes of me staking out the house in so many words, a woman comes out of the abandon house. Not able to entirely see her face, the woman waves to me as to come to her. When I step out of the car the same woman yells from where she is standing "Are you a friend of Angela?" *I nod my head yes while making my way toward her but by the time I make it across the street the woman disappears, back into the house. Not finding an actual opening into the home, I step slightly through a manmade entrance.*

Stepping through the opening I yell "Hello, My name is Beth Morris. Ms. Black – Angela said you wanted to talk me? *No response. I step further into the house and repeat again* "Hello" *But still no response. Stepping in a bit further I attempt one last time repeating who I am. This time I hear shuffling from the back of the house with a flash of light wavering in the air. Startled I put my hand in my pocket to insure my phone was accessible. Checking both pockets, I realize I left the phone on the charger in my car. A sudden flush of panic overcomes me. I begin to walk back toward the opening. Just as I reach the tip of the manmade entrance an average build woman silhouette appears in front of me.*

Where are you going?

I turn and begin to walk toward her voice, not able to see her face due to the darkness Hi Karen.... I was just stepping outside. I realized I left my phone in my car.

Why would you need your phone?

Puzzled by her comment I stop in place. In case my office is trying to get in contact with me.

Don't worry you don't need your phone...

Excuse me?

You heard me. Where you're going a phone isn't needed.

Feeling uncomfortable, I begin to walk backwards toward the opening.

Something wrong Beth? Mrs. Elizabeth Morris.

What? Karen I think I need to come back at another time.

Walking toward me.... No I think right now is fine. *I turn to run towards the opening and I am hit in the back of my head with a very hard object. From the force of the hit, I find myself falling in slow motion face down. All I see is darkness all I hear is throbbing in my head. I'm out!*

Unsure of how long I've been on conscious, I'm awakened by voices, two women arguing? And someone weeping. I hear footsteps getting louder and louder in my direction. Trying desperately to unbind myself, both hands and legs are tied, my mouth is clogged by some sort of rag and my eyes covered with tape. Why is this happening? Who are these people? I begin tugging – pulling at my restraints but the more I try to free myself the hold on my wrists and ankles become tighter.

Oh our guest is awake. How are you this fine day?

…………………

Oh let's take that nasty rag out *pulling the rag out of my mouth, allowing me to breathe a bit easier.* Back to my original question, how are you on this fine summer day?

………………

A kick to my side Mrs. Morris it is impolite not to respond so let's try this again. How are you on this fine day?

…………………

Another kick....... I can do this all day!

Why are you doing this to me?

Kick...... Not the answer I was looking for. Okay then, the next one will really hurt

Good morning

Much better but one problem, no longer morning… Ha ha

Please let me go... Why am I here? What have I done to you?

Done to me? Done to me, let' see, hmmm.... Oh I got one, made my life hell.

How did I do that? I don't even know who you are?

But I know who you are. You're the bitch that took everything from me!

What?

You heard me.

How? I don't know you, never met you before.

Oh but you have. Family functions, dinners… Yes we met many times over.

What family functions - dinners? Who are you?

I never understood your taste in furnishing. A completely white living room, why?

((WHO ARE YOU))

Karen continues to ignore my questions and continues with her review of my home.

And those Dallas / Knots Landing pastel paintings you had hanging in your bedroom and living room. That light skin of yours must go to your head. What, you think ya white?

This woman has been in my home? She is describing my home in North Carolina.

When and why were you in my home?

Oh Beth… Beth… Beth… Beth Morris. You cannot be that damn stupid.

I don't understand....

Of course you don’t, so let me educate you. See you and I shared the same man. Well shared wouldn’t be all that accurate since you and he didn’t have a relationship just a piece of paper. See Michael and I had a relationship before, during and after you. One might say you had my sloppy seconds.

I haven't been with Michael for many years. Whatever you two have, God Bless You! Please just let me go.

You don't need to tell me what you had, I know damn well what you had. I also know what I had before you wormed your way into Michael's life.

With anger in my voice And what did you have?

A man who loved me and his family with all he had until… *Anger building in Karen's voice…* Until you claimed he raped you, until you falsely accused him of beating you.... Oh and wait, that poor unborn baby. BOO HOO!

Unable to control my anger… You don't know a damn thing about me. You don't know how I lived and you do not know the fucking hell I went through with Michael. So Karen or whoever you are, get the facts straight.

Whoever I am? I would be fucking carful with the way you speak to me because this second, right this second I'm your worst nightmare. But who I've been the past nine years, Mrs. Karen Morris, wife of Michael Morris and before then, anything and everything he wanted and needed. That is who the fuck I am.

Good for you Mrs. Morris. I applaud you.

With a swift kick to my left side I will not tolerate disrespect Beth.

Tears forming in my eyes due to the pain (((((((STOP)))))))!

Stop? Oh no we are just getting started. See Beth I don't want to kill you without you knowing exactly why. That just wouldn't be fair now would it? See I had the pleasure of fucking your man every day and every night. Oh yes. He loved me with all he had. You… Oh you. He didn't want you. But you knew how to play on his emotions.

This can't be happening.......

What Michael and I had was real. Unlike you, having him marry you under false pretenses.

You do not know what you're talking about.

I don't? Really? Did you not spread your legs with hopes of having his child within weeks of meeting Michael? Hmm what do they call woman like you? Bitch? Whore? Slut? What?

Please just let me go.

How many times do I have to repeat myself? No plan to let you go. I can't do that. See before I kill you.... Yes that is correct kill you I want you to suffer like I had for so many years.

This cannot be happening Can you please tell me how I have directly hurt you?

Hurt? Beyond hurt..... You took life from me.

What is this woman talking about?

Do you remember Thanksgiving 1988? Well I'm sure you do. See that night, Michael came to tell you he was divorcing you immediately because we were expecting our third child. All you had to do was put your big girl panties on and take the information like a real woman. But instead, in your typical dramatic way you had to put on that charade, attempting to take your own life. How did that work for you?

Karen, Mrs. Morris or whoever you say you are, you want Michael you have him. I don't want him...

AND HE DID NOT WANT YOU. But you, you that night you just wouldn't let him leave, would not let him go. In return you made false allegations against him? Raped and beat you? You may have convinced some but me.... No, no way. I know Michael in every way. He has never ever raised a hand to me or at me. He has never forced me to do anything I did not want to do.

Bravo to you. How lucky you were. I on the other hand was not that lucky. I often had my ass kicked, punched and slapped and often for reasons unknown to me.

In a loud boisterous tone (((((LIAR))))) You God Damn Liar! *Her loud response is followed by an open hand smack across my face.*

Please stop.

Stop? I'm just getting started

Trying to hold back my anger What do you want from me?

In a whisper Your life! That is all I want. I want you to first feel the pain I felt. Endure what I did, then I'm going to make your Thanksgiving wish a realization, I'm going to kill you. Simple!

My heart begins to beat faster, my body is shaking. Remain calm Beth.... Come on think straight...

So let the festivities begin. We are going to play a little game. The game is called "Who knows Michael Morris best". If you win, I will spare your life for a few minutes longer. You lose, well you die sooner. Oh one little piece of information, in hand I have a few syringes of heroine. For each wrong answer I'm going to inject you. Sounds good? Great! So here we go. First question, and an easy one. Where did Michael Morris grow up?

………..........

No answer?

I hear footsteps walking toward me. I begin to move my body around. My blouse is ripped off and my left arm exposed.

One more time, where did Michael Morris grow up?

Please don't do this... Please.

WRONG! *As she shouts wrong I feel the needle pierce my arm. A burning sensation follows.*

Question number two, for a double dose if answered incorrectly what was the name of Michael's first dog?

………..........

Tick tock tick tock... Time is running out.....

Gus.

That is correct

Question number three... Still playing for a double dose if answered incorrectly, while visiting his grandparents during the summer, which neighbor pool did he most often visit?

What?????

Oh boy, if I repeat the question you will not have any saves in the future... So do you want me to repeat the question?

I don't know.

The correct answer is Johnson's family pool, neighbor to the left of his grandparent's home. Now time for that double dose of goodness.

As Karen walks closer, I attempt to put up a fight. Moving my body around, swooshing across the floor.

Keep fighting me bitch and I will kick the shit out of you...Got it?

I continue my swishing across the floor and as promised I am kicked directly in the back.

With pure anger in her voice Move again and I will kick the holy shit out of you. Do you understand? Now *in a calmer voice* you actually have options. Do you want me to inject in your leg or your arm?

I don't care.

Now you're talking *and in an instant my right arm is injected. I begin to feel sick, my head feels as if it is on fire....*

Question number four, for a triple dose if answered incorrectly. How many children does Michael Morris have?

What????

You're doing it again... but I will give you a pass. I will repeat the question again. How many children does Michael have?

My tongue feels so heavy and my eyes, I can't keep them open under this bondage.

I don't know...

The answer is three beautiful girls, three wonderful beautiful girls.

Barely able to lift my head, I yell "wonderful".

Yes it is wonderful. *In a cheering voice* now wait- wait - wait. The game is just getting good. So from this point on I will ask you the two final questions. If answered incorrectly I will inject you after the game is completely over... Is that ok?

....

Great.... Okay question number five, what are the ages of my beautiful girls?

....

I didn't hear you

I don't know.....

You don't know? Really? How could that be, you held my daughter, saying how beautiful she was. Oh right, I forgot right under your nose I was invited to my now in-laws home. Invited with open arms with no pre-judgments, no questions. And my baby-girl Michael's first child loved and adored. The only hiccup was your marriage. Michael didn't want you to be a problem to me so I was introduced as his cousin. See everyone had to think fast all because your yellow ass showed up one hot summer day.

Through the fog building inside my head I begin putting the pieces together. That Fourth of July I went to Michael's grandparent's home. I remember this particular day not for the gathering but for the massive ass kicking I received from Michael that evening, the beginning of many. Only a few months into our marriage. I never understood the mood change in Michael that day until now, this second.

When I arrived everyone who knew who I was questioned what I was doing there, further delaying my entrance into the house. Michael's mother who seemed up to that point basically tolerated my presence presented overly friendly, even engaging in a conversation with me. I should have known something was going on.

Finally making my way inside his grandparent's house I find Michael in the living room holding and feeding a baby girl. A woman and a young girl maybe nine – ten years old sitting next to him on the couch. The woman seemed annoyed that I interrupted and Michael presenting both nervous and annoyed introduced the woman as his cousin - Karen... Yes I was introduced to his "cousin Karen". When I asked to hold the baby, Michael put her into my arms and the woman on the couch stormed out with the little girl sitting with her. That son of a bitch! I held his bastard child? And my assault that occurred when Michael arrived home that evening was for what? Because I upset his "family day"?

Olivia is my oldest, not Michael's biological daughter but loved by him just the same. Tiffany my beautiful little girl you met that fine summer day and my precious baby girl, my youngest *Karen's voice begins to crack* my baby girl Jasmine born on a date you should know so well, November 24, 1988.

Trying to concentrate, I find it very difficult. Michael became a father to her oldest daughter and he had two more with this insane woman. She was pregnant at the time I married Michael? Another daughter born on November 24, 1988? That date means something to me.... But what is it? I begin to doze.

BANG… BANG… BANG....

Karen begins hitting the wall behind me no sleeping no, no, no...... I need you wide awake, for my last and final question, for 100 points on the board....... Answer this correctly and I will have a surprise for you. Okay here we go, where was Michael Morris on November 24, 1988?

I don't know.....

Oh no surprise... You answered incorrectly. The answer is… drum roll please, with you... Yes with you, you stupid bitch. *The anger returns to Karen's* voice. See he was coming to tell you it was time to pack them bags and run back home to mommy and daddy, all the way back to New York. To tell you he did not love you did not need nor want you. But in your true fashion, you yes you, instead of handling your business like a real woman you pulled the woes me card *in a pitiful crying voice* I can't live without you. I'm going to kill myself if I can't have you, I can't do this alone etc. Such a sad, sad, sick woman! Then to top it off you cut your wrist… Oh poor you. But lucky for you today, I care enough to make sure your eyes are closed permanently and your air intake no more. Ha yup, see I have a good heart. Okay time for the grand finale, how much should I inject.... Hmmm you answered two more questions incorrect and divide that by ten then add seven... Ha, I'm no good at math, let's just inject it all.

Completely frightened I'm shaking uncontrollably. Oh God what is she about to do? Please Lord if I'm coming home please let this be painless, please. She is so close to me right now. So close, I can feel her breath on my neck. Her warm hands take hold of my arm. I begin to protest, kicking and moving as much as I can. Just as I prepare myself to be injected Karen releases me from her hold.

Oh wait a second I should probably close the gaps huh? Okay before I bring you to your final destiny, let's review. See, that night when I gave birth to my baby girl, he was with you. My daughter was born without her father. Then for attention you called yourself committing suicide. Then oh yes the major factor was pregnant? Not even Michael's but wanted to blame it on him? So let me get this right, you were pregnant and no man. Wow... But the part I really want to hear about is who gave you the black eye? Bruises on your face, neck and legs, who? Huh... Well I guess that will be one secret you will take to your grave. So, before your life ends here, feel free to ask me a question or two.

I'm very sorry for anything I may have done or caused. Please just let me go… I did not know about you or your children.

Oh I must have forgotten a few important points. See, Michael was never the same after your charade. He became a bitter nasty fucking drunk. *In a strained voice* so drunk he was driving with my baby girl last May, hit the guard rail and my baby girl was ejected from the vehicle and killed.

I am very sorry.

With pure anger you should be, it was your fault. All of it! This is why the people and the things you cherish so much went away.

It just hit me she killed Rosie and Rosa...... ((((You killed them)))).

Yes me, me and all me. Some of my best work took place that morning.

Why did you, how could you! They had nothing to do with you and your twisted understanding of my marriage.

((((((DID YOU NOT HEAR ME...I TOOK WHAT WAS DEAR TO YOU AS YOU TOOK FROM ME))))).

Barely able to speak did you also break into my apartment?

Yup all me. And that sweet little kitty cat, this is fucking funny. When I picked him up, that sweet ball of fur I said your name and that cute little kitty meowed and meowed. He meowed to the point of getting on my ever last fucking nerve. I had no choice but to shut his ass up. That is when I twisted his little neck. Twisted it completely, 360 degrees. Never knew cats were so flexible. Oh boy what a release. I've wanted to tell someone about this but these days who can you trust? And that cop detective friend, your lucky nothing went on between the two of you because he was going to be next.

This woman is insane Do you hear yourself? You act as if I did something wrong, did something to you directly. I never knew about you and I certainly did not know Michael had any children.

With deep hatred in her voice, you're a fucking liar. You knew! You did everything you could to keep him and that Thanksgiving night was the icing on the cake.

((((YOU DO NOT KNOW YOU'RE YOUR TALKING ABOUT))))

My, my, did I hit a nerve, a sensitive spot? Michael told me everything. To get him to marry you, you cried wolf about being pregnant? Then shortly after the ink was dry on the marriage certificate you told him it was a false alarm?

I don't know what Michael told you but your facts are not factual. Pregnant before we were married? (((NEVER))!! I don't know what Michael filled your head with. He never told me about you or having a child. If he had I would not have accepted his proposal and certainly not married him and that is fact!

Oh please you lying yellow bitch. See Michael has always been about family because he did not want his children's life to be as fucked up as his and you played on that, getting him to marry you.

I'm confused, you seem to know about me and I knew - know nothing about you. *My anger increasing* if anything, wouldn't you be the intruder? The other woman?

The other woman? Bitch you got it wrong… I've known Michael since the age of ten, so don't tell me who the other woman was?

Then why didn't you and Michael get married instead of him marring me? Why did he engage in a relationship with me and obviously while you were pregnant?

Do not speak of my children. Do not!

I'm not… Just trying to understand your thinking? Please tell me why he engaged in a relationship with me while he was with you? Why did he marry me knowing you were pregnant?

You know that answer better than I do.

No I don't please enlighten me.

Watch your tongue, you are really pushing it! You know my skin color did not fit the Morris – Kent approval. But who got the last laugh? I was the one who gave him children, I was the one the family took in, treated like the daughter in law and my daughters both loved and accepted.

All true *I say sarcastically* you did get the better end of the deal. What I received was cold shoulders, bruises, broken bones. Yes you certainly got the better deal.

Oh boo hoo… Here you go again. Poor Beth… But you know what they say "darker the berry, the sweeter the juice". You, oh you sour to the core. Wow sharing this information is such a release for me, a form of therapy one might say. Goodness after today I should be good for a very long time. Okay enough of the small talk. Time to meet your maker.

You know you won't get away with this!

Oh but I think I will.

Ms. Black will alert the proper people as to my whereabouts...

Oh I suppose she will but do you want to hear a little secret? Huh... You're not in the same place as before. We moved locations days ago when you were getting some beauty sleep. No one will find you here. Well, I wouldn't say never, just not in time to save your life. Okay really no more chitchat that is it.

Do I at least get to look you in the eyes when you do this?

Is that a request?

Yes

Well request denied.

As Karen denies my request I'm injected multiple times. Initially fighting as best as I can the heroine hits my system hard and I begin to lose control of my movements. A cold rush feeling covers my body. My hands and feet are tingly. I try to force myself to fight, to stay awake but I have no strength at this time. My chest becomes tight. I find it difficult to breathe. I begin gasping for air. I hear Karen laughing and now two more voices, all laughing? I hear a voice say "rot in hell bitch" and I am kicked in the face and chest. The laughing seems to continue then begins to fade. I close my eyes..... I whisper "Daddy I will see you soon".

Chapter 13
Finally Home

I awake from a strange type of sleep. One of which allowed no dreaming nor nightmares, no images at all. Just a serene darkness with expectations of something more to come. Slowly rising to my feet I take in the scenery around me. I look to the heavens, a sky so blue with traces of white clouds that look like cotton balls. I look down at the earth where my feet are at rest, the greenest grass with sprigs of lilies and wild flowers peeking through. I turn in a circle, completely around. Perfectly manicured trees, bushes and flowers. Every animal that once roamed the earth strolling along together in perfect harmony. The food chain that was once so prevalent is non-existent.

I walk toward the most intriguing sounds, cellos, violins and flutes that bring me to a bench that sits right in front of an open field. My inner self instructs me to take a seat and wait for something. What it is, completely unknown. Patience not often practiced by me comes so easily this very moment.

Time continues to pass, at what rate I don't know. Sitting here with none of life's pressures weighing on me I feel a vitality I haven't felt in a very long time. Content, yes content is how I feel. The feeling of complete serenity fills the air. In this moment I realize I am at the entrance of heaven waiting for a familiar face to escort me finally home. I close my eyes and lift my head toward the skies above and yell "I'm finally home*". In this very moment, I hear my name* "Elizabeth, Beth" *from a familiar voice that has been missing from my daily living. I open my eyes and there he stands, my beloved father. Just as I imagined when this day came, my guide, my greeter, my escort for my final journey is my father.*

With tears of joy streaming down my face Daddy I knew it would be you.

Yes my baby girl, it is me

I recall the last time I saw my dad alive. Barely surviving a massive stroke, my father had a difficult time allowing – accepting help. I saw life leave him each and every moment he had to depend on another. A proud man he was. But the image standing currently in my presence is a man with no imperfections. A man completely rested and free of all his woes and worries. A man who ironically looks as if filled with life. This man, this being, my guardian angel, my father looked at peace.

Daddy I finally made it, I'm home. *Verbalizing these words lifted the black cloud that hovered over me for as long as I can remember. In this moment I feel so alive. Until this moment I walked through life as if I carried the weight of the world on my shoulders, as if I was being cursed with immortality.*

Oh my baby girl, I love you and want you with me but now is not your time.

What? Daddy this is where I belong. Please don't make me leave...

Beth this isn't your time, I can't allow you to stay. You must go back.

Daddy I have no life to live. Please don't turn me away. *Tears begin to fall down my face.* My life is over and it has been for some time.

Beth.... You have so much more to offer so much more to accept.

Daddy I have no fight left in me..... Please...... Don't turn me away. How many times am I going to be turned away? ((How many))?

Beth…

Daddy, why does my requests go unanswered? I've given myself in so many ways. I've played by the rules and yet my reward is remaining in a world where my happiness is non-existent? Why? To continue to be rejected by the one person I want more than anything to love me, care for me? Why? To feel the least respected the least loved? To be rejected time and time again? Why can't I just come home?

Beth you can only come home when our heavenly father says it is time.

Then daddy I would rather suffer in hell then continue to fight a fightless battle. I have no more to give.

Baby girl you have the fight. You must gain the will.

Daddy, Rosie and Rosa was taken from me.

They weren't taken away, just like I wasn't.

*My anger continues to build and expressed through my words (((*what do you call it then)))?

Beth I'm still with you every day of your life. Rosie and Rosa, look at them...

I turn and by my side Rosie and Rosa. Both looking amazing.... worried free, pain free...... I miss both of you... *I begin to weep.*

Beth, don't cry for us. We are fine, never better. For whatever the reason God took us from our living form, unable to walk this earth as you do. But our heavenly father gave us the ability to return and look after our loved ones like you.

I don't understand......

Beth, we all are given a purpose in both life and death. For Rosie and me our purpose was to reinstate your acceptance to love, to be loved and to give love.

And I certainly love both of you but now you're gone. What was the sense of it all?

To show you the strength you gained, to show your ability to overcome.

Sarcastically, did I really overcome?

Beth my baby girl, yes you have. And the times you needed a bit of a reminder, I held your hand. If you needed to be picked up our Heavenly Father picked you up personally and planted you back onto your feet.

Daddy, my faith in God lessens every day I walk this earth. I want to continue to believe in him but how much can one person endure.

Beth turn to me

Excuse me? *I turn as if floating on a cloud, in my presence a being I cannot describe. How beautiful it is. How serene it presents.*

Beth, my child you're never alone. I hear your prayers, your pleas. I feel your hurt and sense your pain.

If you know my pain why won't you take it away?

Because your experiences make you who you are! Your pain and sorrow helps with your molding. Beth you may not understand right now, this very moment, but one day you will. You will look back on this encounter and realize the words I have spoken.

So I have to leave?

You do my child. So much for you to experience, both good and bad.

I can't do this...

You can and you will. Remember my child I hear your every plea, your every prayer and I answer each and every one. It may not be what you expect but the answers you receive guide you toward your bigger purpose and believe me, the work you have done and will continue for me will never be overlooked.

Beth...

I turn toward my father

It is time for you to go. We are all with you.

As my father says the words he puts his hand over his heart... We will meet again here one day. *In a flash my dad, my rock, my strength is gone. I turn around no Rosie or Rosa. I'm standing in this open space all alone..... What do I do next? Someone please help me..... What do I do next???? I close my eyes and begin to pray...... God please I'm so confused, what do I do.*

(((Beth..... Beth Morris)))

....

(((BETH)))... Do you hear me?

As the voice calls my name, my eyes are freed from the tape that hindered my sight.

Beth can you hear me?

I shake my head yes. Opening my eyes I see Kevin in my blurred vision. I feel a smile emerge upon my face. Wow Detective Walker, what took you so long? Did you stop for doughnuts and coffee?

Kevin with tears in his eyes takes hold of my face, strokes my cheek and takes hold of me completely in his arms. We must have been in this position now for at least sixty seconds. When he finally releases me, Kevin looks me in the face and shakes his head. "Elizabeth Morris you are the hardest - headed woman I have ever come into contact with". *His statement followed by another hug.*

Jokingly, Did you miss me Detective Walker?

Every second!

From his words, my eyes fill and tears begin to stream down my face. I am very sorry.

Beth, I'm just glad I found yo*u* and you're alive.

I begin to pull lightly away to look in Kevin's beautiful face. But immediately as our eyes lock on each other Kevin strokes my cheek and kisses me as if this was our final goodbye. Once our lips part Kevin again begins to stroke my cheek. He then wraps and tightens his jacket around me.

Beth are you okay?

I am. No worries. Where am I?

An abandon building. Beth do you know who did this?

She said she was Michael's wife, Karen Morris.

Your ex-husband's wife? Why would she do this?

Kevin I don't know. Can we talk about this later?

Beth??

Kevin I just want to go home.

Beth EMS is on the way. You have to go to the hospital and be checked.

Kevin I'm fine *and as I plead my case to go home, I attempt to stand. Staggering a bit I'm on my feet for less than a few seconds. The jacket that was covering me falls to the ground. Attempting to pick the jacket up, I'm halted in place by the sight of me. Unclothed and completely bare I see what Kevin was trying to cover. I look up to Kevin with tears trickling down my face.* Kevin what happen to me? What was done to me?

Kevin's response comes in the form of tears and taking me into his arms. Before words could be spoken EMS arrives.

Sir please step out of the way. *Kevin still holding on to me ignores the responder's request.*

Ma'am, can you tell me where you are bleeding from?

I'm bleeding? What happen to me?

Ma'am, the needles on the floor?

What?

Ma'am the syringes around you, what was injected?

My speech begins to slur. I was injected with heroine.

As the EMS worker begins to take my vitals Kevin's partner walks over.

Beth, who did this? Do you know the person?

Kevin responds, she said her ex-husband's wife.

Beth do you have a name?

Trying to focus on what is going on around me I try to answer but no words come out my mouth.

Do you have a name? Was she alone?

Her name is Karen. I thought I heard more than one person.

What did she say to you? What was discussed?

Hearing the question I attempt to answer. My words are slurring even more. My vision completely blurred. I hear one of the EMT's say she's coding.... *I'm out.*

Chapter 14
The Beginning of Something

Beth how are you feeling today?

Much better Dr. Jacob, with that said please tell me I'm being released today?

Before Dr. Jacob's could respond standing in the doorway, Kevin and my loving sister. In unison "Don't start Beth"

Beth once we get updated test results we may be able to discuss a discharge date. Until then, what your family said *and with a smile Dr. Jacobs leaves.*

Beth I thought we agreed no more discussion of discharge until Dr. Jacob's has spoken of it?

We did Kevin, but

NO BUT MISSY…

Cynthia, I'm going on day five in this place. I'm ready to go home.

I don't care if it was day thirty. When your doctor says you are ready, then you are ready to go home. Until then, "zip it"!

As if pouting… Whatever…

Kevin, do you mind if I have a few words with my sister?

Sure Cynthia, Can I get you something from the cafeteria?

No, thank you.

Beth, can I get you anything?

Giving Kevin the look of... please don't leave me with her... Kevin says with a smile "I will surprise you" *and leaves the room.*

How are you feeling?

I'm doing fine Cynthia.

What test results are pending?

More cultures, blood etc. *Knowing what the next question is going to be I answer before Cynthia inquires.* It is assumed no sexual assault occurred. Penetration yes but that could have been from activity I engaged in a few hours before. *I know my face is beat red discussing this with Cynthia* and no seamen.

Thank God Beth!

Yes I am thankful. But enough about me, any family gossip?

Beth, don't start! We need to talk about this.

Cynthia what do we need to talk about?

I called Michael and his mother.

Why?

Why… Really?

What is there to talk about? What, I married a liar and a cheat? That his whole family willingly supported him in his lies? I get that.

Beth…

Cynthia no, let's not talk about this.

Beth, you were left for dead! You were severely beaten! You were drugged, so drugged up that you went into cardiac arrest.

I guess telling her I actually died, talked to daddy and met God would only play into her belief in my need for psychiatric help. If anything I appreciate the people in my life even more. But to dwell on this, I don't want to do. Cynthia I can't. I started meeting with a counselor here yesterday and I will continue until I feel it is no longer necessary. But for now Cynthia all I want to do is get back to a normal routine, sleep in my own bed and go to work. If I don't I know I will dwell on all that has happened, who has been taken away from me and what could have been my demise.

Beth do you know why you have a police officer outside that door?

Cynthia don't!

Because, that sick bitch hasn't been found. *As the wrath of Cynthia begins a tap at the door...*

Come in... *I reply immediately with hopes of whoever is at the door, will interrupt this conversation.*

Is everything alright? *Kevin inquires as he enters.*

My sister needs some reassurance that I'm safe and no longer in danger.

Beth... *Kevin says, no longer smiling*

Oh come on, not you too?

Beth...

No Kevin, time to change the subject.

No Beth, this is a good time for a reality check. *Kevin glances over at Cynthia as if obtaining approval.* Karen Morris has yet to be found. Both New York and North Carolina have APB's out. When State Police searched your ex-husband's home, boxes of evidence was carted away. Cut out pictures of you, pictures of you here in New York, of your apartment, your cat and *(Kevin voice cracks)* Rosie. Notes/captions reflecting how she feels about you! Certainly what was found expresses her dislike for you. Police also found items from your wedding, a matchbook, napkin and a wedding favor. When your ex-husband was questioned, he stated he didn't know about any of the items found. He also informed the officers of his wife leaving him about six months ago with his daughters and hasn't seen nor heard from any of them since. When inquiring why Karen would want to come after you, he stated his wife felt you ruined their lives.

How? *I ask after even though I know the answer*

He couldn't or wouldn't tell the officers but when I met with his mother yesterday, she stated Karen felt you were the cause of her daughter's death.

Exactly what she said to me

Seems over the years Michael became a heavy drinker. His mother says shortly after you lost the baby he began to drink, blaming himself.

This is a joke…

Beth this is what she sated. Last May Michael and his youngest daughter were driving from North Carolina to New York. Unfortunately a tractor trailer hit them head on. The girl wasn't wearing a seat belt and was ejected from the car. She was pronounced at the scene. Since then, you have been the brunt of her revenge, repeating too many she was going to take away the things you love as you did to her.

As Kevin repeats her statement, a cold chill goes up and down my back. So what does this mean Kevin? I will not be a prisoner in my own home.

For now Beth, you will have police oversight and no argument.

Kevin, she had her revenge. She succeeded with taking close people away from me. I doubt she comes back after me.

Beth, you may be right but what she intended to do didn't completely go as planned, hence you talking to us right now. Until we have this woman in custody, please adhere to my request, please!

Kevin's request leaves no other words to be said. I'm even surprising myself with no rebuttal, no argument. The room goes silent for several minutes. I look over to Cynthia who appears tired – worn out.

Hey Cynthia please go home and get some rest.

Beth I'm fine

No, you're not. I see it all in your face. Go home and get some sleep. I promise I will stay put.

Kevin interrupting me

And I will make sure she stays put. Cynthia I'm off tonight and will stay here.

Beth are you sure?

Cynthia I'm very sure.

Alright I will call you later this evening.

Okay Cynthia. *I kiss my sister and home she is headed.*

Once Cynthia leaves Kevin excuses himself, taking a phone call. Relieved to finally having a few minutes to myself, I lay back, close my eyes and try to focus on anything but my life. Hard to do when you know someone has been watching your every move and the possibility of her still doing it sends a sense of fright over me. But in that same thought I begin to sympathize with Karen. Losing her child the way she did. I begin to tear. Michael the cause of all of this. Who knows what he told Karen. Needless to say the lies. I can only imagine what lies Paulette spread regarding Michael and my breakup. Even bigger lies told on me since that Thanksgiving Day occurrence popping up in the police blotter section of the newspaper I'm sure. That's small town America for you.

I can only imagine what story was concocted to justify to friends and family. Based on Paulette's inability to come to terms with what her son did to me, losing the baby as she stated to Kevin. I can only imagine what Karen was told. I'm sure she was told that my allegations of physical abuse was all false. Michael physically and verbally abusing me was all in my head. In her mind, it never happened and certainly did not cause me to lose a child. Trying to think of anything but this I begin to surf the channels, keeping the TV on the news. I begin to doze and finally sleep.

Daddy, stop crying. I haven't given up… Please daddy stop crying I haven't given up.

Beth, wake up. Beth…..

Huh – What? *Waking from a deep sleep*

Are you alright? You were crying in your sleep.

Wiping tears away I'm fine, just a dream. What time is it?

Five thirty in the morning.

And I woke you up, Sorry.

No I was up.

You need to go home and get some rest.

Beth I'm fine.

Just as I am about to debate the issue with Kevin, a nurse comes in.

Good Morning Beth, Dr. Jacobs's called and good news, your being discharged this morning.

I begin to laugh... He called this early? He really must be tired of my request to go home.

A small chuckle actually he is already here. He had several emergencies late last night and early this morning.

Oh okay *I say as I am getting up to pack*

Beth slow down, Dr. Jacobs still needs to write your orders.

I would rather be ready to leave the second he writes them *I say with a smile.*

I will put everything together for Dr. Jacobs. We will try to get you out in the next hour or so.

Great I really do appreciate that.

Once the nurse exits the room Kevin looks at me and says "Beth you will still need to rest when you get home".

Not wanting to argue the matter, I politely shake my head and continue to pack.

Finally discharged! How good it feels to be home. Stepping into my apartment I am greeted by Tiger. Oh I missed you little man. *Kevin carries my bags into my bedroom and Cynthia continuing her motherly fuss, trying to steer me directly into my bedroom. It seems like a lifetime since I've been home but in actuality it's been nine days. Nine days of hell.*

Beth I turned your bed down and laid out your night clothes.

Cynthia, taking a rest right now isn't on the agenda. I've been on my butt for several days. All I want to do is take a hot bath, check my voice mail and then some paperwork.

Minus the bath, you can do all that in bed. I will run your bath.

This is going to be one long night! Cynthia I appreciate the offer but I can do it. I wasn't put on bed rest.

No but Dr. Jacobs did outline what you need not do for the next few weeks – until you return to him for your follow-up.

In a frustrated tone Cynthia I am aware of the do and don'ts. With that being said both you and Kevin need to go home and get some rest. I'm home now and promise not to leave.

I guess I just told the joke of the century because they both burst out in a loud laugh.

Ah yes Beth, we know how well you follow direction … oh so well! *Turning to Cynthia* for the next few days I'm working 2nd shift. I can stay overnight to late morning. Any way you can stay until I get off?

Listen both of you, go home and get some rest. I'm not in need of babysitters and I need to get back into my normal routine.

Completely ignored Cynthia and Kevin continue to engage in their own conversation.

Yes I can

Hello, I'm right here? Now both of you go, please!

So Cynthia do you need anything from the grocery store?

Very funny! *My frustration increasing*

Beth, plan is set. Cynthia will stay with you this afternoon and I will stay this evening.

Whatever! *Feeling defeated, I go into the bathroom to run my bath. While walking into my bedroom to obtain a change of clothes I find Cynthia and Kevin in a low voice conversation. Both with a look of worry.*

Hey you two want to let me in on the secret?

Startled by my entrance, Cynthia and Kevin abruptly end their conversation.

Are you two going to share?

Beth nothing to share. I was just asking Cynthia if she wanted me to pick her up anything from the store before I left.

Really? Whatever!

Beth, can I get you anything before I leave?

No Kevin

Okay then I will see you this evening. Cynthia there's an unmarked car parked across the street. If you need anything call my cell.

You be safe Kevin

I will Cynthia. And Beth *walking toward me in my bedroom* I will see you this evening. Do not be a pain in your sister's butt.

Hmmm I see you and Cynthia have gotten closer these last few days.

One, your sister is good people. Two we have something in common.

And what might that be?

YOU! *Kevin says with a serious look* Yes you *and I am kissed on the forehead.*

Blushing I hope the kiss on my forehead is only the beginning!

Beth……

Just asking… *Putting my arms around Kevin I kiss him on the lips and whisper* You give me something to look forward to. Thank you!

Baby from the first time I laid eyes on you, you put a beat back into my heart. *Kissing me passionately on the lips Kevin pulls away* I will see you this evening.

Be safe Kevin….

I will no worries *and Kevin is out the door.*

After my bath I find Cynthia preparing what she calls a light lunch. But the heavenly scent coming from my kitchen screams "Soulful Sunday Dinner" not "light lunch".

Cynthia I know many of the ingredients used to make this heavenly meal did not come from my kitchen.

Beth, you're absolutely right about that. When was the last time you shopped?

Believe it or not…. not too long ago. Actually the day I came to see you.

Cynthia laughs I think I need to teach you how to shop.

Wow, kick a sister when she is already down. *Both Cynthia and I laugh.*

So Beth, good time to talk about Kevin?

What is there to talk about?

You and your games, how serious are you two?

Cynthia nothing serious, you know I don't do relationships.

Well it seems Kevin is into you.

Cynthia when I have something to report *I say with a smile* you will be the first to know.

For the rest of the afternoon Cynthia and I watch trashy talk shows that we couldn't tear away from. Discussed family and friends and discussed books we both recently read. Cynthia an African American literary junkie spent several minutes scolding me on my lack of familiarity of black writers. Although she and I have a common like for Walter Mosley and Terry McMillian, my knowledge of these two authors isn't enough for my sister. By the time our so called literary debate ended Kevin was at my door to relieve Cynthia.

So how did you two ladies spend your afternoon? *In response I chant* "Jerry – Jerry". *In unison we all began to laugh. Cynthia who seems to be head over heels crazy for Kevin prepares a plate for Kevin, catering to his every need. The two of them present as old friends, family even. Cynthia's likeness for Kevin adds a few brownie points to his score card.*

As the evening comes to an end, Cynthia heads home with the promise of returning tomorrow. Every effort made to get her to stay home but I am once again defeated by the super duo. Preparing for bed I give Kevin the option of staying with me or finally getting a good night sleep by way of my couch. Relieved that he opts for sleeping with me, Kevin and I lay in bed. Kevin starting a new novel, something more he and Cynthia shares – the joy of reading and I watch whatever is on TV. But my TV watching is short lived. The comfort of being in my own home, own bed and feeling completely safe, I very easily fall asleep in Kevin's arms. For my first night back I find pure comfort being home, in bed with the man I last shared it with.

Chapter 15
Thanks and Giving
Thanksgiving – 1999

The transition from summer to fall is just about done. The hot days of July and August are being replaced by autumn's dormant preparation. Already Thanksgiving I awake this morning with both excitement and apprehension. The excitement of spending this day with people I love. Grateful, well for the obvious... Grateful to "want" to see another day! Appreciating more my relationship with Cynthia and having Kevin in my life. My apprehensions, my inner battle focuses on my insecurity with my life as a whole. Sometimes an obsession, I can't shake the feeling that something more is about to happen. My life and its events present more of the calm before the storm. What the storm is I'm completely oblivious to but the uncertainty leaves a sense of incompleteness, unsettlement. Maybe knowing Karen is still out there, not yet caught fuels this feeling. Warrants issued across multiple states. The news media depicts her as a cold stone murderer with determination to continue her path of destruction.

Luckily throughout all of this I was never identified by name. Only those close to me knew who the news reporters were referring to when reporting on the "incident". I was known as the "unidentified caseworker with a local domestic violence not for profit agency". Thanks to Kevin information provided to the media was very limited and generic. The only details provided a description of Karen and what she is capable of.

As I continue my daily self-check, I hear my front door close. My heart flutters with the idea that Kevin is "home". I can't believe I am allowing myself to feel this way, like a teenager with a new boyfriend. But I can't help it. For the past few months not once has Kevin and I been out of each other's presence for more than twenty-four hours, not once. Who knew? Certainly not me! If anything I convinced myself to just go with the flow and whatever this "thing" is, to ride the wave until it hits land. At least this way I would have control over self and not go to that dark place I've managed to stay away from over the past few months. Surprising myself, I find each morning being grateful to open my eyes to another day, to live. But even more amazing - a perk, being grateful to wake up next someone who I believe loves me for who I am with all my baggage, to have someone accept me with my flaws. To have someone try new things just because I express a likeness or interest in it. I smile at the thought of this tall, caramel tone handsome man's now likeness for Elvis Aaron Presley. Can you believe it? I think he has purchased every movie sold on tape. And my music choice, to actually listen and seemingly enjoy songs like A Less Conversation, Pork Salad Annie, Born in the Ghetto and the kicker Amazing Grace all sung by Elvis.

Good Morning Beth

Good morning Kevin. Why didn't you wake me? I would have prepared you something before your run.

Wake you? Not even a thought. I love to see you sleep. I can watch you for hours.

I have the feeling you have already!

So my lady, what's on the agenda for today?

Well I know someone is expecting to see you today. Probably wanting to see you over me!

Never, you know you're on the top of her list *Kevin says with a smile.*

Yeah sure *and as I begin to climb out of bed I am grabbed by the waist and pulled on top of Kevin.*

Detective Walker I like where this is leading.

Take your mind out of the gutter missy.

Oh okay *I say with a smile and while rising to my feet.*

Where are you going? *Kevin inquires with a puzzled look.*

Well you stated my mind was in the gutter so I assume no hanky panky today.

In an instant I am pulled back on top of Kevin. Do you know I can hold you in my arms for hours?

Kevin with you this close to me I can't think of anything other than praying you will take me…

Take you where? *Kevin says with that devilish smile.*

Take me to that world of pure physical bliss.

Really?

Really!

Well I'm here to please your every need *and his words are followed by a very passionate kiss. I begin my voyage to the land of complete bliss.*

After a perfect, idyllic and pleasurable morning, Kevin and I finally make our way to Cynthia's for

Thanksgiving. Arriving early enough to provide Cynthia with my limited kitchen abilities, I assist by setting the table. The one positive trait if that inherited from my mother, proper dining etiquette and by the look of this table the apple did not fall far from the tree. Unfortunately or fortunately, is this the only trait inherited? Beth we aren't traveling down this road today. No pity party. Over the past few months I've done so well not to dwell and fixate on this subject. My mother being any subject of discussion has only been in the presence of Chris, my therapist who I've been seeing weekly since the incident. Through my sessions I've been able to let go of the animosity that was brewing daily months back. I questioned how a mother couldn't feel any maternal feelings. Could not visit her daughter or call during a time where death was a great possibility. Could not and do not understand but through therapy I am learning how to cope – deal with this form of rejection. Hmmm enough of this subject. The table is now formally set and dinner can now be served.

I look directly into my sister's eyes and mouth from across the table "I love you". Tears begin to flow down my face. Reminded of what occurred months back and how differently the outcome could have been. Cynthia responds with an intense nonverbal stare, she too begins to cry. Tears now flowing down each of our faces, we both begin to laugh.

Grabbing my hand under the table and wiping my tears away with his free hand, Kevin whispers "I love you" *then stands and request the attention of all seated at the table. Looking over at Cynthia, tears begin to trickle faster. This is the first time Kevin has expressed his love for me verbally. Over the past few months if it seemed the conversation or verbal expression was going to be made I found a way to skirt away from the subject, changing the subject completely. But today, this very moment he managed to sneak it in and instead of avoiding I embrace the words, the expression. I find myself in this moment to be open to the sentiment. The fear I had with allowing myself to not only love another but a man to love me seems to be no more. I allow my heart to skip a beat at the sound of his name. I allow my heart to be vulnerable to another, to him. I on this day after so long of not allowing myself to be in love, look up at Kevin and whisper "I love you too". With a smile now larger than life Kevin continues.*

Cynthia, I want to thank you for inviting me to join you and your family on this wonderful Thanksgiving Day. Usually I am the first to volunteer to work on holidays. My captain was in complete disbelief when I told him I was taking today off. But when he realized I was spending it with you *Kevin looking down at me* he like others who knows me says "I'm a man in love", something I do not need to be brought to my attention. *Pushing his chair back away from the table Kevin is now on bended knee with a box in hand. The room is silent. Not able to remove my stare from his eyes, Kevin motions for me to look down to the box in his hand.*

Elizabeth Cook, our initial meeting was not under the best of circumstances. But from that day although tragic, something wonderful came from it, you came into my life. You're the piece of the puzzle that has been missing. You… *(voice cracks)* complete me. Elizabeth Cook will you marry me?

In this moment I find myself now looking at Cynthia who is both crying and smiling. I look back down at Kevin. Seeming as if my response is taking forever I close my eyes and eternally question if this is right for me. Daddy, I know you're witnessing this. Do I go down this path again? Could I be happy? Does this man really love me? Please daddy, help me with this decision. And just then, as if he is giving his approval personally an old broken clock that belonged to my father begins to play one of my father's favorite songs - Darling You Send Me. Cynthia knowing me sometimes better than I know myself says

"Question answered now answer Kevin's".

No longer hesitating, no longer questioning, letting go of my fears I stand, push my chair away from the table and meet Kevin eye to eye on bended knee. My tears flowing like a faucet left on.

Kevin loving another… I never thought I could allow myself. Having someone love me back, I assumed could never happen. But when my world was turned upside down you entered my life like a glove to a hand. I never thought someone would come along and complete me but you Kevin you did, you do in every way I need. Yes Kevin I will marry you.

With tears streaming down his face Kevin in one swoop hugs and kisses me. I love you Beth.

Okay do you plan to put the ring on her finger? *Cynthia says through her laughing and crying.*

Was just about to do that.... *Taking the ring from the box Kevin places it upon my finger.* I love you *and Kevin plants one more kiss.*

Sitting back at the table Cynthia stands and requests that everyone raise their glass.

To my soon to be brother in law, my brother I welcome you to the family with open arms. My sister, my daughter, and my baby girl I am so happy that you're finally getting what you deserve, happiness and love. To both of you, *glasses raised* many years of happiness. Communication the key, keep it flowing and your relationship will continue to flourish.

Dinner resumes. Old stories told and memories of my dad shared. Kevin learning how dysfunctional my family is, one would think by the stories told he would be heading for the door. But instead he remains here with me, by my side. Conversation throughout the afternoon and evening stayed away from the elephant in the room, my abduction. A subject I have basically banned anyone to speak of in my presence. Not oblivious to the what if's... I know what could have happen and what actually occurred. I am aware of the realities of who has been taken away from me just five months ago. Bottom line, I'm alive and for once in a very long time grateful to be.

Beth… earth to Beth

Hey Cynthia

I hope you were lost in the land of wedding planning and not anything else.

Yes… Yes I am *just a small white lie*

Are you taking in all the good that has finally come your way?

I'm trying Cynthia.

Trying? No trying, let it flow through you naturally. Reason for the hesitation?

I don't know Cynthia. I haven't been this happy in such a long time. I love Kevin and want to spend the rest of my life with him but I feel uneasy, like something is about to take any and all my happiness away.

Beth it is normal to feel this way with all that has happen. Once Karen is in custody we all can breathe a bit easier.

I guess…

I hope you're not questioning Kevin's feelings for you because Beth, h*e* loves you. You hear it in his voice, you see it when he looks at you and I saw it personally when we thought we lost you.

I know Cynthia. I just hope daddy approves.

Did you not hear daddy's approval? How many years has that clock sat on that mantle and not once played a tune? You received daddy's approval I'm sure of it. So when are we going to start planning?

Cynthia, no plans needed. Quick trip to City Hall will do the trick.

City Hall?

Just as Cynthia discredits my idea Kevin walks in.

I'm with you Cynthia, City Hall Beth?

City Hall is exactly what I want.

Then if that is what you want it is what I want.

Well then you too will have your way with where you get married but I will have all say in regards to the reception.

Oh Cynthia, nothing big. You know me small and simple.

Sure Beth… we will revisit this conversation tomorrow. By the way what do you two have planned for tomorrow?

Kevin is working and I was going to spend the day home.

Change in your plans. You come by tomorrow and spend the day with me and Kevin can meet you here after.

Cynthia you already did all this today.

Yes and I have enough food to feed an army. So it is set, I will see you both tomorrow.

Ending the evening, Kevin and I say our goodbyes. At the door, I hug my sister with my normal bear clinch. While wrapped around her Cynthia states "You deserve it all and I want you to enjoy it all". *Cynthia and I then exchange our usual I love you(s) and Kevin and I leave.*

During the car ride back to my apartment I begin to think about how I spent the last few Thanksgivings, all with Rosie and Rosa. It's been at least five years since I had a sit down dinner with Cynthia and my nephews. I would usually pop in later in the evening, once dinner was done. But this year going to Cynthia's was my only consideration. The past few months having my sister more involved in my life helped me gain the strength needed to face another day. All that I assumed I did not want nor need in regards to that mother figure, came to a close when my loving sister not only took care of me in this recent bout of need but especially during a time in my life when I had no hope and no longer wanted to fight to live. In this moment I realize what I always had.

Chapter 16
An Old Tradition No More

The day after Thanksgiving, a day I would often look forward to beginning in September. But this year, just another day on the calendar. I didn't pick-up on Cynthia's insistence of me coming by today until now. She knows what this day means rather meant to me and she knows what is no longer. I sit here on my couch and scan my living room. I begin to picture what would have been.

Rosie and Rosa arriving around noon. In the kitchen chocolate chip and sugar cookies baking in the oven. On top of the stove, a large pot of hot coco made from scratch. Yes this is what would've been. I continue my look back but now visualizing, feeling as if it was happening right this moment. I can smell the cookies baking and the chocolate from the coco. I hear sounds of Christmas playing on the radio. I close my eyes and see Rosie struggling with putting one of many ornaments on the tree. I see Rosie now sleep on the floor with Gizmo tucked under her. Rosa singing silent night in Spanish while putting the finishing touches on the gingerbread house. But back to the here and now tears begin to trickle down my face. My Thanksgiving tradition started some six years ago just relived in less than five minutes and now gone permanently. What was, is now forever gone.

As I continue down the road of no more my thoughts are interrupted by the phone ringing.

Hello

Hey Beth, are you on your way?

Hi Cynthia, no I'm just staying in today.

Oh come on Beth, I already begun reheating everything.

No I'm sorry Cynthia *and just as I begin to defend my stance for staying in, a knock at the door.*

Hold on Cynthia someone is at the door.

Who is it?

Your sister! *Sounding as if I should already know who it is.*

What? I open the door and there she is, my loving sister.

Funny Cynthia, what are you doing here?

I knew you weren't going to come to my house today so I packed everything up and I came to you.

Cynthia, thank you but no thank you. My plan is to just lay around and read.

Well I guess you and I will be doing it together *and Cynthia steps in.*

So where should we start?

Start what?

The decorating of course!

Oh not today Cynthia.

What?

Just not into it this year.

Wrong answer! You started a tradition and you should keep to it going. No better way to honor their memory than doing what you all did together.

Cynthia I don't know.

Well I do. So I need to get a few things out the car. I'll be right back.

A smile emerges upon my face. Maybe I can do this. I go into the kitchen to see if I can pull anything together. I open the cupboards, no hot coco, but I do have tea. I look to see if I have all the ingredients for cookies. Unfortunately not. I'll run to the supermarket. I go into my bedroom and begin to pull off my oversize night shirt. I hear Cynthia in the living room.

Beth can you give me a hand?

Sure just changing my clothes *and as I am ending my sentence and entering the living-room I am stunned by what I find.*

Cynthia????

Like I said, you couldn't make it to the party so the party came to you.

Please tell me you did not buy all of this?

No I didn't. But your soon to be husband did.

What?

I think you have the one man in the world that actually listens to what you say. *Cynthia says with a smile.*

I don't recall telling Kevin about *and just in this moment I recall a conversation Kevin and I had one evening shortly after being discharged from the hospital. Laying in bed Kevin asked how I spent my holidays. Unsure of where he was going with this I asked why? His reply was* "The passion and excitement I hear in your voice when you talk about the last few Christmases spent with Rosa and Rosie". *But in the same conversation he inquired why I felt so different about New Years. The best way I could explain it was the false promises made at 12:00 a.m. on New Year's and by Noon on the same day forgotten about. Kevin, seeming to know when not to pry any further in that moment leaves my explanation un-dissected.*

Hello Beth… Earth to Beth

I'm here. So what is all this?

Everything we need to keep your tradition going.

Cynthia...

I don't want to hear anything. So let's get this party started.

Cynthia and I throughout the afternoon baked cookies, listen to Christmas music and decorated the kitchen, living room, dining room and bathroom. By the time we were finished it was already six p.m.

Beth are you cracking up? Laughing by yourself?

No Cynthia, I just know how much you love me in this moment.

How?

For you to actually decorate for Christmas before December 24!

I'm not that bad Beth.

Oh you are. But I love you for this. Thank you!

Not needed. Always remember the best way to honor those that have passed is by doing what you normally do. They would want that.

I agree

Just as Cynthia and I have yet another bonding moment, we hear keys opening my door. Like two teenagers, smiles emerge upon both our faces, Kevin is home.

Hey my ladies, how did you two enjoy this day?

Based on Kevin's greeting, it dawned on me he and Cynthia set this up. He wasn't surprised to see her here.

Your ladies are doing just fine *and I kiss Kevin* But why do I get the feeling you two had this day preplanned?

If we did or didn't did you enjoy?

I certainly did.

Good. But it isn't over yet. I have a small surprise to keep the evening going. *Kevin goes back out the door. After a few minutes he returns with a beautiful, tall live Christmas tree.* Will this do my soon to be wife?

Absolutely! *I say with a larger than life smile.*

Great, let me change and we can get this trim a tree party going.

While Kevin is changing Cynthia has already set the table, reheated the food and placed it on the table.

Cynthia why only two places set?

Because this is my cue to leave.

Please stay and at least eat with us.

No, this is time for you and Kevin. Wonderful to keep a tradition going. Even better to start new ones!

Kevin comes back into the dining area now wearing NBA Knicks shorts, a tank and barefoot. This man is stunning in anything and everything he wears. Sexy as hell in suits but absolutely delicious looking in his workout attire. Hey you two, why only a setting for two?

Because I have indulged in this Christmas thing enough *Cynthia says with a smile and a wink at me.*

Whatever my loving sister. But thank you for today. It will be my pleasure to return the favor next Saturday at noon. I will be by with bells on.

Oh no you won't

Oh my sister I will. You could never turn me away.

Laughing always a first time.

Cynthia now with her coat on is approached by Kevin, taking the bags she has in her hand away.

I'll walk you out Cynthia.

Cynthia call me when you get home!

Hugging and kissing my sister, I whisper "I love you"

I love you too Beth. I will call you when I get home. And Beth, enjoy the rest of the evening… Enjoy!

Cynthia and Kevin exit the apartment. I go into the kitchen and grab two wine glasses and a bottle of wine. Placing the items on the now set table I walk over to the window to see if Kevin was heading back inside yet. Not only has he not come back inside but presenting to be in deep conversation with Cynthia. The Cherrie mood they both exited the apartment with seems no more. They both revert back to the look of worry. Cynthia now hugs Kevin and she is off. Kevin heads back into the building.

Everything okay Kevin?

Yes, yes it is Beth….

Then why the worried look?

No worried look Beth… Now let's eat so we can get that tree decorated.

Decorate tonight?

Well isn't that the tradition?

Well yes, but it is already late and

No Beth, you will not get out of this one. We will eat then trim the tree. I've been looking forward to this all day.

You're such a fibber *I say with a smirk.*

Eleven p.m. Kevin and I are stretched out on the floor in front of our beautiful decorated tree. I turn to my side and look Kevin directly into his eyes.

Thank you for today.

No I should be thanking you Beth. I can't tell you how many years it's been. Decorating for the holiday's I haven't done in many many years.

And why is that?

Because it is only me. Don't get me wrong I at least hang a wreath on my door.

I chuckle and could that be because you pay dues to the condo board and annually the board hangs the wreath?

Ha ha my lady you are absolutely correct.

Just sad Kevin *I say while laughing*

Well I have you now in my life to condition me to the holidays

Kevin you do know the holidays are for the young.

Well young at heart I will always be and if we have children I will experience through their eyes.

From Kevin's last statement it seems the conversation is about to go into a different direction. Kevin seems as if he has something to ask and I know I want to know his take on children, something that has been weighing on me for some time, since his proposal.

Kevin, I don't know how to even begin

Beth, begin what?

Rising to an upright position a discussion about children

Beth?

Kevin you and I never discussed having children *tears begin to form*

Sweetheart, why… what is wrong?

Kevin you and I should have had this discussion before I accepted your proposal.

Beth, stop!

My tearing now a waterfall You know I was pregnant once before and you know how well that turned out.

Beth you don't need to

Interrupting Kevin Yes I do. The relationship between my own mother hasn't really been a mother daughter relationship and from that experience, children….. I never wanted to put someone through that.

Beth, I never met your mother and I don't know what relationship the two of you had but I have met the woman you told me raised you and I know her morals, compassion and love were instilled in you.

Kevin, I can't take that chance.

Can't take a chance?

Kevin you don't understand, I don't know if I can give someone that type of love.

What about Rosie?

I chuckle while crying My Rosie was different, she was special.

And any child you have will be that as well.

Kevin, all I'm saying is, I understand if you want to resend on the proposal.

Beth have I told you how stubborn you are? I love you. If we have children great, if we don't, I have you. Children no children, it is you and me.

Kevin

BETH, *taking me into his arms* all I ask is that you review how you feel with your therapist.

In that moment, conversation on the subject ends. I look into Kevin's eyes and whisper "Did I tell you how much I love you"?

If I get to hear it again, no you haven't.

I love you my soon to be husband.

I love you, but I can't wait to drop the soon to be.

Well let's fix that

Really?

Really Mr. Walker!

And what would be the plan?

Kevin you're off next Tuesday we will go down to City Hall and apply for the certificate.

With excitement in his voice AND

And, we will have the license on hand, we will be one step closer.

What a tease

No, no tease. How about January 02 at City Hall.

Are you sure Beth?

Very sure!

Then we have a plan *and in that moment Kevin rises to his feet and extends a hand to hoist me up. Once I am on my feet Kevin then swoops me off my feet.*

Kevin what are you doing?

Practicing for the honeymoon!

We both laugh and off to bed we go.

Chapter 17
The Beginning of a New Me
January 31, 1999 – New Year's Eve

Heavenly father as I look back on the last few months of my life, what has occurred, relationships gained and love accepted without false pretenses I want to thank you. You saved me not once in my life but twice. Maybe not grateful then, but certainly grateful this very day. But with all my gratitude father I have one more request. Help me get through this day. Let me enjoy this day to the fullest and not allow me to dwell in the pool of pity. Let me get through this day with happiness in my heart and not bitterness. I beg you heavenly father. Daddy, Rosie and Rosa I love and miss the three of you. Help me through this day.

Good morning my soon to be wife, I didn't realize you were up.

Good Morning my soon to be husband.

Wow I love the sound of that but I can't wait to be just your husband.

Kevin you will never be "just my husband"! *I say with a smile.* What time will you be leaving for work?

Six, so we practically have the whole day to spend together.

Yes I guess.

Hey I thought we talked about this?

Kevin I'm fine, no worries I promise.

And you're sure you don't want to go to Cynthia's to ring in the New Year?

Nah… Tiger and I will stay right here and ring it in together.

Just make sure you're not on the phone especially around midnight. My goal is to ring in the New Year with my soon to be wife one way or another and if that means by phone, so be it.

You don't need to do that Kevin. If you can't call I will be just fine.

Just as Kevin was about to probably debate the issue his cell phone rings. He leaves the bedroom. Tiger who is curled up next to me begins to purr. Yes my little man it is you and me tonight. *I pick up the TV remote and begin surfing the channels. Kevin returns to the room with a bleak look.*

Is everything ok Kevin?

Ah… yes Beth. Unfortunately I have to go in earlier.

How much earlier?

I have to leave out in a few. Beth I am really sorry.

Kevin no problem, Tiger and I will enjoy our day in bed.

Beth would you please consider going to Cynthia's? Please! *Kevin asking this time is much different than just before. This time the request comes with the tone of you will do this and accompanied with a look of please just adhere to my request. But because I am who I am and all that this day comes with , new year – fresh beginnings and all those false promises by way of resolutions I stay true to myself and commit only to here, where I am at – Kevin's apartment.*

Beth I really would prefer if you stayed with someone.

Nope, I'm good right here. Now you go ahead and get out of here.

Soon to be Mrs. Walker, my soon to be wife… *Kevin says with an enormous smile* I love you.

I know you do and I you. Now get out of here and let me and my little man enjoy some TV.

Ok but Beth, no going out and lock the door!

Kevin I thought we got passed this. For today – tonight yes but reminder, I return to the office next week. No more working from home, no more restrictions regarding my field work – home visits etc.

Don't remind me Beth.

Hey, *I say with a smile* I followed all the rules as promised but I have to get back to life.

I understand Beth but

No buts Kevin and enough of this. You get to work. Be safe. I will be right here waiting for you.

I love you Beth *and Kevin's last words are followed by the door closing. Kevin leaves and that lonely feeling begins to set in.*

Come on Beth don't do this. The only way I will be able to shake this feeling is to sleep the day away. I get up and grab two sleeping pills from my purse. I go into the kitchen for a glass of water. I open the cabinet and take down a glass then go to the refrigerator to fill it with water. When I'm about to open the refrigerator I find a note tacked to the refrigerator door.

Beth I know this day is going to be especially difficult for you. Just wanted you to know I love you with all I have and here for you. Also know that your dad, Rosie and Rosa are with you in spirit, you're not alone. Love, Kevin.

Oh Kevin, so far I was able to suppress my tears but you had to write this. I love you too. I pour myself a glass of water and return to the bedroom. Sitting on the side of the bed I take the letter that Rosa wrote me prior to her death and place it under the pillow. Since receiving this letter only once has it been out of my sight and that was when, yes that day. But since, I always have it with me. I take the two pills and begin surfing the channels again. Nothing like a Twilight Zone Marathon on New Year's Eve. Picking Tiger up and placing him onto my bed, we both lay down. I begin my New Year's Eve avoidance slumber.

Approximately 9:45 p.m. I am awaken by the phone ringing.

Hello?

Beth?

Um yes…

Beth sorry to wake you

Mrs. Frankel is everything okay?

No Beth, a bathroom pipe burst in the Jackson's apartment above you and we think your apartment is flooded.

Oh you're kidding me. Okay I'll be home in about fifteen minutes.

Okay Beth, see you soon.

This is all I need. Should I even bother to dress? Nah, I'll just throw on a pair of sweats. I guess I should at least wash my face and brush my teeth. Okay Tiger let's go. I won't leave you here alone. *Almost out the door I remember I left my letter under the pillow. I go and retrieve the letter and place it into my purse. Okay now I am ready to head home.*

Less than ten minutes later I am home. Shit where am I going to park, no spaces anywhere. Someone in the building must be having one hell of a party. Circling the building once more I find a space about a block away. Well no other choice. Tiger locked away I grab the carrier from the passenger seat and begin walking to my building. Once arriving I immediately smell something amazing cooking. I guess I should have been a bit more social with my neighbors, if so I could have probably knocked on a door and requested a taste. But unfortunately this evening that is not the case. I guess Tiger you and I could order a pizza after the cleanup.

Arriving at my apartment door, that amazing smell seems stronger. What a cruel joke. I unlock my door and step in. When I flick on the light to my amazement, my apartment is completely decorated with beautiful flowers – yellow, white and pink roses everywhere. A long table is taking up part of the living room. I now know where that amazing scent was coming from. Then it hit me, I'm standing in my apartment not alone but with familiar and new faces. Some family some friends and a few unknowns, all formally dressed.

Ah what is going on?

Wow you really know how to dress for the occasion.

Cynthia what in the hell are you doing here?

I asked her to be here.

Kevin what the hell and why are you dressed in a tuxedo? And looking absolutely FINE…

Well Beth, if I remember correctly someone special in your life requested that from this New Year's on, you celebrate like it is your last, to seize the day and enjoy yourself. What better way to accomplish that you ask? Our Wedding! A new meaning, a new way to embrace “New Year’s Eve”!

What? Wait I thought we agreed on City Hall? *Not giving anyone time to answer* No I can’t do this. I’m in sweats… haven’t even showered! *From my last words I hear laugher from about 40 people. Taking Tiger’s carrier from my hands Kevin* leads me into my bedroom.

Kevin what did you do?

I didn’t do much. This is all Cynthia. I told her what I wanted to do and she took care of the rest.

Oh Kevin, are you sure you want to do this tonight?

I’ve never been surer of anything. Do you want to marry me?

With tears streaming down my face Kevin I have *never* been more certain of anything. I love you Kevin Walker…

And I love you. So let’s get this show on the road. *Kevin opens my bedroom door and gestures to Cynthia to come in.* Cynthia she is all yours. *Kevin then kisses me on my lips and leaves the room.*

So Beth where should we begin?

Begin? Begin with what?

Well you just announced to a crowd of people that you haven't washed your ass today so maybe a shower?

Oh so my sister has jokes!

Not a joke, get your stinky butt into the shower.

Both Cynthia and I begin to laugh.

Luckily I have an entrance to the bathroom from my bedroom. I begin my shower and undress. While in the shower I keep asking myself if this was really happening. But in the middle of my inner debate over if I should do this or not a tap on the door.

Beth?

Cynthia come in.

Are you almost done? We have a schedule to keep to.

Really! *I say with a tone of sarcasm.*

Really Beth! Come on let me help you out.

I got it Cynthia… By the way who did you invite?

The normal.

Cynthia you know where I'm going with this.

Beth I did invite her but

Feeling like a damn fool for even bringing her up Forget it Cynthia no need to explain. *As I walk back into my bedroom I see a garment bag hanging on my closet door.*

What's in the bag?

I guess you will need to open it to find out.

Unzipping the bag my eyes begin to swell. Inside the bag is a beautiful off white A-line gown. A gown I had told Cynthia was beautiful from a picture in a magazine. A gown she stated I should have and I said absolutely not due to the cost and more obvious, overkill for a city hall wedding.

Cynthia, *tears falling down my face w*hat did you do?

I purchased my daughter her gown. That is what I have done. Nothing out of the ordinary, this is what the bride's family is supposed to do.

Oh Cynthia it is beautiful. I will pay you back. I can't let you do this.

Now you just insulted me.

Oh… *tears falling* I love you.

And I love you. Now, I have waited a long time for this day.

Cynthia, should I remind you that I've taken this walk before?

Actually you haven't. You're getting married to your soul mate. The person you complete as he completes you. Big difference! Enormous difference, colossal difference, vast difference!

Alright, alright *I say with a smile* I get the picture. Ha I guess I can't forget you did not want me to marry Michael. You knew something wasn't right.

Hmmm no need for the "I told you so"… *Both Cynthia and I begin to laugh.*

Okay Beth, a friend of mine is here to do your hair and makeup. *Cynthia opens my bedroom door and motions for someone to come in. When he enters I begin to smile with tears falling.*

Benny you?

Yes girl. I'm here and it is Benita.

Ha ha… But I recall your mom calling you Benny. How are you?

Hugging me tight. I'm fine my little peach. When Cynthia told me you were getting married to a good man I told her I would be the one transforming you into the Princess you are

Princess why not queen?

Because Mama Cynthia will forever hold that title. So let's get this party started. Cynthia out! Only room here for two.

Leaving the room, Cynthia winks her eye at me. The only reason I am leaving is because I know you're in good hands. *Then my bedroom door is closed.*

Feeling as though Benny and I have been in this room for hours it actually has been about one hour. Fully dressed now, Benny has insured that both hair and makeup are perfect.

Tap… Tap…

Come in as long as your name doesn't sound like Kevin.

Door opens Crazy girl it is only me *and as Cynthia walks towards me she is halted in place.*

Beth *with tears trickling down her face* you're absolutely beautiful.

So Miss. Cynthia I did well huh?

Benny you did great.

Well can I take a look? *I walk to my closet door and open it to reveal my full length mirror. Amazed by what I see, I begin to cry.*

Beth come on, why are you crying?

Laughing and crying because I never looked so beautiful before.

You're wrong. Beth you have been my beautiful princess from the day you were brought home from the hospital.

Now you're going to make me do the ugly cry…

OH NO NO NO honeys both of you stop. We don't have time for a do over.

The room engulfs with laughter, so loud we missed the first few knocks by Kevin.

Hey are you guys having your own party in their?

Not without you my soon to be husband.

Well then, get out here so I can finally drop the soon to be.

Cynthia with a big smile on her face responds, Hey hold your horses you have the rest of your life with her.

Oh alright, but can you make it quick.

Kevin's answer comes in the form of laughter and Cynthia opens the door and hugs her soon to be brother / son in law. Get everyone ready and she closes the door.

Beth I hope you like your bouquet. Arranged by Kevin!

My bouquet, made up of White and Red roses with Casablanca lilies and orchids, all my favorite flowers.

I love it.

Okay you should head out.

But wait, Cynthia where's your bouquet?

What?

Cynthia do you think I am getting married without you my Matron of Honor, Mother of the Bride and last and not least the person giving me away?

Beth come on, we don't have any time for this.

Oh yes we do. I pull a long stem red rose from my bouquet and hand it to Cynthia. Now if you don't mind, please take my hand.

In this moment I hear Sam Cooke loud and clear singing "Darling You Send Me". Beth hold back the tears. Cynthia grasping my hand even tighter, she too probably trying to hold back tears not only for what is happening but for daddy, wishing he was here to be a part of this. To see that I am finally happy.

Cynthia and I step out of the room hand in hand. I see Kevin and only Kevin with a radiant smile upon his face. Seeing him makes me want to run to him rather than walk. Cynthia and I walk hand in hand, finally arriving to the appropriate standing position. Cynthia releases my hand and places it into Kevin's. She whispers "I love you" *kissing both Kevin and me and moves to the side of me.*

Kevin and I now stand in front of one of Kevin's friends whom I met about two weeks ago. An ordained minister Kevin grew-up with. Never imagined our meeting would lead to this.

Kevin and Elizabeth you stand here in front of family and friends, in the presence of God and all those who have left their earthly form as witnesses to the union of each of your single lives to one. When the request was made to officiate over this union I looked into Kevin's face, into his eyes and saw he is a man in love. Then I met Elizabeth and instantly I understood how my friend since childhood was happier than I have ever seen. When Kevin told - not asked *chuckles from the crowd* I was conducting this ceremony this evening I asked Kevin how the two of them met. What I learned from a very simple question is what I have always believed in. Out of tragedy new life, new beginnings emerge. Not always blatant, sometime obvious but a belief. This evening, tonight is proof of this.

Elizabeth and Kevin marriage is a sacred vow between a man and a woman. Quoting Proverbs Chapter three verse five and six: "Trust in the Lord with all your heart and lean not on your own understanding. In all thy ways acknowledge him, and he shall direct thy paths". Kevin and Elizabeth, as written keep your faith in the lord. When troubled, confer with thy God then communicate with one another. Although the two of you have been tested in so many ways, the future will not be without. Communication and Respect are the bases for any true marriage and you too are already off on the right track.

So with no further ado, Kevin Jackson Walker, do you take Elizabeth Lillian Cook to be your wedded wife, to live together in marriage?

I Do

Do you promise to love her, comfort her, honor and keep her for better for worse, for richer for poorer, in sicknesses and health, forsaking all others and be faithful only to her, so long as you both shall live.

I do.

Elizabeth Lillian Cook, do you take Kevin Jackson Walker to be your wedded husband, to live together in marriage?

I Do

Do you promise to love him, comfort him, honor and keep him for better for worse, for richer for poorer, in sicknesses and health, forsaking all others and be faithful only to him, so long as you both shall live.

I do

Then by the power instilled in me by our heavenly father and the state of New York I pronounce you husband and wife. You may kiss your bride.

Not giving Derrick time to finish, Kevin and I look into each other's eyes and instantly kiss.

When they decide to come up for air, I would like to introduce Mr. and Mrs. Kevin Jackson Walker.

In that instant, the room erupts with hand clapping and laughter.

Everyone please grab a glass. 10, 9, 8, 7, 6, 5, 4, 3, 2, 1 *Cynthia leading the toast* Congratulations and HAPPY NEW YEARS

Kevin turns to me with tears forming in his eyes. But tears for what? The look in his eyes this very moment express more than joy but fear, an emotion I haven't seen from Kevin before.

My wife I hope tonight met all the expectations of an unforgettable New Years?

Mr. Walker, my now husband I know Rosa and Rosie are here and they are both pleased with how I spent this day. I also know my dad is here in spirit and gave his blessing. He too knows you're the best thing that has ever happened to me.

So anything I do or say this very moment would be accepted with open arms?

Mr. Walker what are you trying to get at?

Mrs. Walker the honeymoon and the plans I made begins in *Kevin looks down at his watch* seven hours and twenty-five minutes.

Kevin what are you talking about?

Be ready in seven hours and twenty-five minutes!

My voice now sounding strained Kevin what are you talking about?

We are on our way to a nice tropical island for a week.

(((What)))) Kevin I can't, I did not prepare for this nor did I clear this with Rochelle.

And just when ending my statement Rochelle comes to where Kevin and I are standing.

Beth *kissing me on the cheek* you look absolutely beautiful and Detective you're not too shabby either *shaking Kevin's hand.*

Thank you Rochelle, glad you could make it. I really miss you guys and I can't wait to get back into the office.

And we can't wait to have you back. Matter of fact, no time like the present to tell you of my resignation.

What? Why?

A position became available at the Mayor's office - Committee on Domestic Violence.

Congratulations Rochelle I know you have wanted this for some time. Wow will not be the same without you.

Well you would never guess who the board appointed as the next director?

Oh boy… who?

Rochelle and Kevin exchange looks and now smiling. Rochelle answers with a chuckle

YOU!

Kevin now kissing my forehead congratulations Beth!

Wow Rochelle thank you. *I then turn to Kevin* Why do I feel you already knew about this?

I just found out about it earlier today when I called Rochelle about our trip.

Rochelle I don't know what my handsome husband told you, but I will report to work on Monday as planned.

No you will not. When Kevin called to inquire about vacation time and his surprise I was thrilled to hear that you were actually getting away. Plus with your promotion it will be at least a few months before you will feel comfortable enough to take off. I know you too well.

Rochelle I can't

Oh you can, you will and finally I have the last word.

Laughter erupts from the three of us, sparking Cynthia's curiosity, she walks over and inquires what she had missed.

What's going on over here?

Rochelle my sister Cynthia, Cynthia Rochelle.

We met already Beth and took the opportunity to talk about you.

Thanks Cynthia

Your welcome *my loving sister replies*

I guess you have been informed of Kevin's surprise trip?

I have and I think it is fabulous.

You would Cynthia

Turning to Kevin what am I going to do about clothes? Bathing suit? Clothes in general?

My lady no worries, Cynthia did some shopping and what you don't have we will purchase.

What about Tiger?

What about him? He and I will have a good time at my house.

Cynthia really!

Enough of your excuses woman, I would like to dance with my beautiful wife *Kevin extending his hand for mine. Once again I feel myself blushing like a school girl.*

I'm all yours my husband *and in that moment I'm whisked into Kevin's arms. Dancing ever so slowly to Nat King Cole, I rest my head upon his chest.*

Kevin whispers in my ear "I love you" *I begin to melt.*

I whisper in return, I love you too my husband and I can't wait to make love to you as Mrs. Kevin Walker, your wife.

Smiling there is a difference in the love making?

Well I couldn't give it all to you. Some things need to remain sacred.

Well I say party over, better yet let everyone continue to celebrate and we can go back to our apartment.

Ha ha we are in "our" apartment!

Another area we need to work out when we return *Kevin now with a serious look on his face.*

It will all work out Mr. Walker. But right now all I want is a kiss from my very handsome husband. If you don't already know, I love you with all my heart, my prince charming. I waited a long time for you and I look forward to spending the rest of my life with you.

Beth I have waited my whole life for you. You were the missing piece needed to complete my life. Now that I have you I promise to GOD, Jesus Christ and your father to always protect and keep you safe.

With his last words Kevin pulls my head upwards so that we are looking in each other's eyes. Looking into Kevin's eyes my heart sinks a bit. So much pain on his face, worry and his eyes glossy from held back tears.

Kevin is something wrong?

No Beth just overwhelmed with your beauty.

That was a great answer but not the truth. Kevin are you okay?

Beth I am more than okay. I have you in my life and I could not ask for anything more. Now enough of the questions woman. Let's rush this evening so I can get you into one of our bedrooms and allow you to make love to me now that I am your husband.

Wow the excitement… Hope I do not disappoint.

No I hope I never fail or disappoint you!

Kevin, I have one request

Anything Beth

Don't be so quick to agree

Beth

From this day forward I promise to say I love you when I first wake next to you in the morning. I will say I love you before closing my eyes at night. In times of anger, I want each of us to promise that before either of our bodies lay to rest we will remind the other of our love and never allow anger toward one another to fester.

Beth I do promise. You are my Queen and you will be treated as such. I love you Mrs. Walker my wife.

Tears begin to fill my eyes I love you too Mr. Kevin Walker my husband. Now let's finish up this party. Only a few hours before we take off and I need to show my husband what I have been holding back.

In the voice of Elvis Aaron Presley "How Mercy"!

We both laugh

I love you Mr. Walker!!! Always……

Phone Calls

Detective Walker this is Detective Harris with the Greensboro Police Department.

Yes Detective Harris, it's been awhile. How can I help you?

A body was found this morning off interstate 73, not too far from Greensboro. We are waiting on dental confirmation but it is believed that the body found is Karen Morris.

What was the cause of death?

Will not know until the medical examiner completes the autopsy but Walker, if it is the remains of Karen Morris we have bigger issues.

Why?

Based on an on scene look by the medical examiner the body is almost twelve months post.

What? That can't be. That means……

So now you understand the dilemma!

Yes I do. When do you expect confirmation?

Hopefully, by the end of the week. As soon as the results come in I will let you know.

What about her daughters?

Still missing. The father claims he hasn't seen nor heard from any of them.

Thanks for the call.

Walker? Harris.

Find out anything?

Ah yes. Body found is Karen Morris.

……… and?

What we feared. In its decomposing state it is believed that the body is ten to twelve months post, leaving even more questions.

Harris – cause of death?

Heroin overdose

Self-injected? Suicide?

Walker we believe she was killed and evidence shows her body was dumped where found. Whoever dumped her body covered their tracks pretty damn well. The area very isolated.

Oh my god this can't be.....

Walker are you still in contact with Beth Morris?

After a long sigh... In contact, ha we will be married this evening.

……….. Congratulations but I suggest extra security.

Any word on her daughters?

No, still missing. Her husband still sticking to his story! Says he hasn't heard from any of them for months.

Autopsy shows any sign of a struggle? Any DNA found?

No, like I said whoever is behind this covered their tracks fucking well.

I appreciate the call. Please let me know if anything more comes up.

Walker you do the same and again congratulations.

Thanks!

Ericsson, Walker here

Hey man, getting ready for the big day?

Something like that

What's up?

I just hung up with Harris from Greensboro, Karen Morris was found about a week ago.

Man isn't that good news?

Not at all, her body was found and it's believed body is post ten to twelve months.

What?

Exactly!

What about the daughters?

Still missing

What the fuck man, any ideas?

None. I've been playing this over and over in my head and no results.

Are you going to cancel tonight?

No, everything to go as planned. But… just come prepared.

Not a problem. I will also pass it along.

Thanks man.

Listen don't worry. For today, tonight enjoy yourself. Too many of us will be around for anyone to try anything.

I hope that is the case but one factor remains, we have no idea who is behind any of this. Up to an hour ago we knew at least one of the suspects, pretty cut and dry. Now we are back to square one and Beth nowhere near safe.

Listen man, you do what you need to do to prepare for this evening. Beth still has a car at her place?

Yes… Unmarked and she is unaware. I'm headed down to the station now to look at a couple of things.

Alright I will meet you in twenty.

Ericsson you don't need to. I just need you bright eyed and ready for tonight.

Don't worry man my tux is ready for my Best-Man role!

Yeah okay. I will see you tonight.

Actually I will see you in twenty!

Hello

Cynthia, ah we have a situation

Hey Kevin, what is wrong?

………………

Kevin?

Cynthia Karen Morris was found. Greensboro Police think she was murdered.

Oh… I will say a prayer but I am so thankful that we can stop walking on egg shells.

Cynthia *Kevin's voice sounding concerned* it is believed she was killed ten to twelve months ago.

Okay great, but why are you sounding so *and in midsentence, Cynthia yells* (((What did you say)))?

You heard me correctly

Kevin this can't be

Unfortunately Cynthia it is. I wish it wasn't. I'm headed down to the precinct but Beth is at my place as planned.

Kevin should we cancel?

No Cynthia, everything will go as planned. My partner will make sure security is tight and I'm adding a second detail.

Kevin if Karen is dead and has been then who killed Rosa and Rosie? Who is after Beth? Why are they after her?

Cynthia I wish I had the answers. But Cynthia I promise you I will keep Beth safe.

Kevin I don't doubt that. Did you speak to Beth about this?

Cynthia she has plans to return to work on Monday.

I know but have you talked to her?

No I haven't.

Kevin, I know my sister and how freaking pig headed she can be but you need to sit down and talk to her. She can no longer be dismissive regarding this matter. She needs to understand that someone is out to kill her. Kevin she needs to know this.

Cynthia I know and I will.

Kevin, I know you are doing all that you can to protect Beth and keep her safe but with this new information she needs to know. Right now it could be anyone she knows. *Cynthia now sounding as if she is trying to hold back tears* Kevin why is this happening? She has been through so much… For the first time in a very long time my sister is happy.

I know Cynthia

No Kevin you don't understand *Cynthia's voice muffled by her crying* Beth before any of this shit starting has gone through so much, often times not feeling worthy to… She's just been through so much. It has only been the last few months, since you that I can say my sister is truly happy. But enough of this, today is both you and Beth's day.

Cynthia I will have a very long discussion with Beth and update her with all that is happening but I would rather wait until tomorrow. I want Beth to enjoy this evening.

What about you? You're the other half of this evening.

Cynthia I will be just fine. I will rest better once this person has been caught.

We all will.

I'm heading down to the precinct now. Call me if anything at all comes up.

Kevin I will. Be safe!

Hello

Hello…… *sighing deeply* I need your help

How can I help?

I'm getting married this evening to a wonderful woman

……… Congratulations

But………

Talk to me

A few months back, Beth, my soon to be wife was abducted and left for dead. The threat is still immanent.

I'm listening

Who was assumed to be responsible was found dead and believed to have been murdered almost a year ago *voice cracking* I need your help to keep Beth safe.

All will be taking care of. I will make all the necessary arrangements. To start, what are your honeymoon plans?

We didn't plan to take one.

Well now you are. I will make the arrangements. I will call you back within the hour with your itinerary.

Beth doesn't know about…

I assumed she didn't. The planning and travel will be discreet I assure you.

Thanks and I apologize for not inviting ….

Interrupting I understand why you didn't. I'm just glad you called me now. …. I will take care of everything and call you back within the hour.

ABOUT THE AUTHOR

Elizabeth Cook-Howard is a wife and mother to four beautiful children. A resident to the Lower Hudson Valley Region for more than thirteen years, her passion to write began in her early teens, while growing up in Queens, New York. Facing forty-five years young she decided to conquer a long time goal of penning and presenting her fictional stories to all interested, hence the Forever Beth Series.

www.ingramcontent.com/pod-product-compliance
Lightning Source LLC
Chambersburg PA
CBHW071302170626
46809CB00001B/319
* 9 7 8 0 6 1 5 8 2 4 8 3 3 *